Major League Shutout

Major League Shutout

by Terry O'Reilly

jms books

MAJOR LEAGUE SHUTOUT

JMS Books LLC
10286 Staples Mill Rd. #221
Glen Allen, VA 23060
www.jms-books.com

Printed in the United States of America

ISBN: 9781483920801

Chapter 1

THE THUNDERBOLTS HAD just won both games of their doubleheader. It was kind of a big deal as the Bolts were currently in last place, not only in their league but in all of major league baseball. They had just beaten the Yankees—the previous year's World Series champions and the team with the best record overall—twice in the same day. From the way most of the players were acting, anyone would think they'd won the Series instead of just a couple of mid-season games.

Obadiah Benson, the Bolts catcher, made his way to the showers through the crowd of players and reporters in the locker room. His parents had chosen to name him Obadiah—which they'd always told him meant "Servant of God"—because they had insisted he would one day follow in his father's footsteps and become a preacher. But Obadiah, as soon as he was old enough to protest, at about age three, had tossed out the moniker and hung the nickname of O.B. on himself, declaring he was going to be a baseball player and that no self-respecting ballplayer would be called Obadiah. O.B.'s parents had lamented over his choice of nickname and career. That is, until O.B.'s high-powered salary in the major leagues started providing lucrative supplements to his father's meager income as a Southern Baptist minister. Suddenly God's will for their son had been revealed: Baseball was his true calling. Even though his mother still refused to call him O.B.

None of the reporters paid much attention to O.B. as he walked by. The throng from the media was clamoring for interviews with the two pitchers who had played that day, as well as Jake Robinson and Neil Carter, the right fielder who'd hit back-to-back solo home runs in the ninth inning. Robinson and Carter had been pivotal in winning the second game, which had gone to the bottom of the ninth with the Bolts behind by a run with two outs on the board.

The physical and mental strain of being involved in every defensive play wore O.B. down over a long season. It had a negative effect on his offensive output as well. He knew he wasn't a great hitter or a fast base runner; catchers rarely were. The power hitters and pitchers got most of the attention. That didn't bother him. His low-profile position was just fine. He'd let the other guys grab all the publicity and glory. He didn't want his name and face all over the news.

He dropped his towel on the bench outside the shower room, walked in, turned the knobs, and let hot water run over him. His legs ached. He was only twenty-six, but playing nine innings in that crouched position was hard for a man his size, and eighteen innings was pure torture. After his shower he'd head for the training room and the whirlpool. He was well aware that if he wanted a long career in the majors, he had to take care of his body. Maybe he'd ask one of the trainers for a massage—that was, if he could make sure it wasn't Haskel. Haskel was just too hot.

The man had all the characteristics that pressed O.B.'s buttons: tall, blond, blue eyes, smooth muscled body, and only a hint of body hair. When Haskel worked on him, O.B. had to lie on the table an extra fifteen minutes before he could get up without embarrassing himself. And there'd been one time when he'd been so horny he'd actually cum on the fuckin' massage bench while Haskel was working on him. No, he'd make sure it was Jenkins or Albertson. They did nothing for his overactive libido. He'd be safe with them. Unfortunately, his thoughts of the upcoming massage and Haskel had caused his cock to start to tingle and come to attention.

Fuck! You horny bastard. You gotta get yourself laid tonight!

As he exited the shower and grabbed his towel to cover his tumescence, O.B. noticed one of the media guys, a young reporter, smiling at him. He turned his back on the nosy prick and made his way to the training room.

Once there, he dropped the towel and stepped into the swirling waters of the hot tub. He sat, leaned back, and let out a huge sigh; the hot eddies caressed his tired muscles and helped him relax. However, he was still having trouble convincing his cock that this was neither the time nor place to get stiff and demand attention. Remembering the time he'd been in the training room alone and had stuck his dick into one of the tub's jets, letting it get him off, didn't help one bit. But it was like trying not to think of a white elephant on the coffee table once someone in the room said that there was one there.

Fuck, he thought, *no one's gonna think I'm horny because of some trainer workin' on me. Every one of the guys on the team will have sex on their minds after wins like these. Their testosterone is gonna be pumpin' through their veins and makin' them just as hot to trot as me. The married guys are gonna fuck the brains outta their wives and the single guys are gonna be on the prowl for some willing groupie-cunt. So what the fuck. I got a woody. I'm just on the make like any straight guy. Only what I really want is my hard cock in some hot dude's ass, not some bitch's pussy. But no one's gonna know that but me.*

After twenty minutes of soaking, O.B. got out of the tub,

dried off and, wrapping a towel around himself, walked out into the training room. There were about a half-dozen players being worked on for various post-game aches and pains. Haskel was working on the right elbow of one of the pitchers.

Perfect, he's busy, O.B. thought. He looked around for Jenkins and Albertson. But they, too, were occupied, working on players. O.B. briefly considered skipping the massage, but his hamstrings hurt badly enough that he knew he'd have to have it if he was going to be able to play tomorrow. He headed for the far end of the room, away from Haskel, hoping Jenkins or Albertson would be free soon. But just as O.B. passed the table where Haskel was working on the pitcher, the handsome blond called out, "O.B., I'll be done here in a jiff. Hop up next door and I'll be with you in a minute."

"Oh, crap," O.B. muttered.

"What's that?" Haskel asked over his shoulder as he continued to massage the pitcher's arm.

"Ow! Cramp," O.B. said, covering his verbal ejaculation and limping to add to the subterfuge.

Aware that ignoring or refusing Haskel's offer to work on him would seem strange, even rude, O.B. climbed up on the adjacent training table, lay down with his hands behind his head, and crossed his legs at the ankle. He tried to think of something that would distract him enough so the embarrassment of the time he'd shot his load while Haskel had worked on him wouldn't be repeated.

O.B. closed his eyes and began to doze off. He'd successfully gotten his mind off the sexy trainer by thinking of the next day's game—mentally reviewing the relative strengths and weaknesses of the starting pitcher with whom he'd be working. He was brought back to full wakefulness when he felt a firm hand clasp his left quad just above the knee and give it a squeeze.

"God, you catchers," Haskel said. "You got the legs, man. So, tell me, Mr. Benson, where does it hurt?"

Haskel continued to lightly massage O.B.'s thigh as he waited for a response.

Feeling his cock starting to get in on the action, O.B. quickly turned on his stomach and said, "Tendons. Really tight today."

The trainer ran his practiced hands the length of each of O.B.'s hamstrings from the knee to just below the swell of his bubble butt.

"Yeah," Haskel said matter-of-factly. "I can feel those tendons wantin' to knot up and that's putting a lot of pull on all three hammies. I'm gonna get the vibrator. Be right back." The trainer gave O.B.'s butt a playful smack and walked off, snickering.

"Fuck! The vibrator," O.B. mumbled into his arms as he lay facedown on the table.

He didn't know what the technical name of the instrument was, but they all joked about *the vibrator* and how it could get a guy off in thirty seconds flat if he wanted to use it on his cock. It stimulated blood flow to muscles and tendons by using ultrasound vibrations, and it produced a very pleasant sensation as it did so. *Feels too damn good!* O.B. thought. *Shit, might just as well give up and enjoy it. I'm half hard already.*

Haskel returned. "All set?" he asked, but didn't wait for a response before lifting the towel, laying it across O.B.'s ass, and slathering his legs with a cold gel. That was followed by the application of the vibrator, up one leg and down the other. "Spread 'em a little, O.B.," Haskel requested.

O.B. obliged. But the spreading exposed his nuts, which got a good dose of the pulsations from the machine when Haskel brought the vibrator up to and around the base of his ass and between his legs. "Holy shit!" the catcher exclaimed.

Haskel laughed. "Feels good, don't it?"

He purposely put the device in contact with O.B.'s balls and laughed again.

"Cut it the fuck out!" O.B. said, squirming to get away from the pleasurable sensations that were running from his good-sized balls to the tip of his dick. "I'm gonna fuckin' cum!"

"You wouldn't be the first," Haskel chuckled as he moved the vibrator away from the sensitive area and back down O.B.'s leg.

For twenty minutes the tantalizing torture continued. Each time the machine was brought up to his nads, O.B. was sure he was going to shoot. But in the end he held his load.

The vibrator was followed by a massage. O.B. didn't know which was worse in terms of the turn-on it produced. Haskel warmed sweet-smelling lotion in his hands and, with firm, even strokes, kneaded and manipulated O.B.'s well-developed hamstrings. Once again he was sure he was going to cum as his body was rocked back and forth from the rhythm of Haskel's massage. His steel-hard cock was pushed against the leather of the training table as he thought of the stud massaging his legs. How he managed to avoid blowing his load he didn't know.

Now, as he sat leaning against the wall, his legs draped over bags of ice, he wondered if Haskel might not be getting an extra bonus from the job he did with the hunky ballplayers. He watched the man as he worked on another of his teammates, but couldn't decide whether or not the guy was getting a charge out of the intimate contact he had with the athlete's sexy body or not.

Don't matter. Even if he is gay, I'm not gonna take a chance on screwing around with anyone who knows me and knows I'm a ballplayer. There's no way you can be out and still be in the major leagues. No way at all.

O.B. WALKED INTO the dimly-lit bar. The Out and Proud was his favorite gay hangout. He thought it ironic that the name of the place he enjoyed the most was in such juxtaposition to his situation: He was anything but out. But it was the classiest gay bar in the city. The others were sleazy and seedy. He felt much more comfortable here, even though the name belied his own status.

Rock music was playing as he made his way through the Saturday-night crowds to the bar. He checked himself out in the mirror behind the shelves of liquor. He decided he looked pretty good, his tight-fitting black tank top showing off his buff frame with his deep, muscular chest and thick biceps. He ordered a beer, turned, and leaned against the bar.

Let's see what's on the menu tonight, he thought, sipping his drink and surveying the crowd. O.B.'s sexual preferences weren't set in stone. He knew lots of guys liked one particular type over others, but for him it depended on his mood. He could get it on with hairy, chubby older guys as well as smooth, slender twinks. Some days, although rarely, he had an appetite for muscled, body-builder types like himself. Other times he preferred average Joes who just needed to be fucked. He appraised the crowd on the dance floor, trying to make up his mind about what would satisfy his needs this night.

He caught sight of a young man looking his way. The guy had an inviting smile and a handsome face.

Mmm, nice, O.B. thought, looking the kid over. He knew the establishment carded the customers, but this guy didn't look like he could possibly be of age—*eighteen maybe. That wouldn't be legal in here with alcohol being served. So he must be at least twenty-one,* O.B. thought again as he watched the guy dance. The kid continued to look in O.B.'s direction and it became clear he was flirting. The dancer smiled, winked, turned his back, and wriggled a very nice, full ass in O.B.'s direction. O.B. decided the twink was worth encouraging, so he smiled back, nodded, and lifted his glass in salute.

The boy seemed to take a deep breath through puckered lips, then raised his hands over his head as he undulated in a slow circle to the beat of the music, running his lips up and down his own bicep.

Hmm, looks like he works out. O.B. felt his attraction to the young guy grow. *But how the hell old is he, anyway?*

The song ended and O.B. watched as the kid made his way off the dance floor and approached. As the guy got closer, O.B. became aware of how short he was. *Can't be more than five-seven or -eight. Bet he doesn't weigh more than a hundred-thirty drippin wet.* O.B.

mentally compared that with his six-foot-five, two-hundred-and-fifty pound frame and found that, for tonight at least, the size differential was a big turn-on.

"Hi, I'm Chuck," the guy said, sliding in between O.B. and the man standing next to him. There wasn't much space, so Chuck wound up being pressed against O.B. The boy's head came up to just below O.B.'s chin, his chest tucked under the bigger man's own, with O.B.'s hardening cock squeezed against his stomach.

The man standing next to them looked over his shoulder, shrugged, and moved away from the pair to give them more room, but Chuck didn't move at first. He just stood and looked up into O.B.'s face with a big smile on his full, pouty lips.

O.B. returned the smile and said, "Hi yourself, I'm Sam."

"Hi, Sam. Nice to meet you," Chuck said, finally moving back slightly.

"How old are you anyway?" O.B. asked over the loud music.

"Wanna see my driver's license?" Chuck retorted, faking a pout. Then he called to the bartender over O.B.'s shoulder. "Hey, Tim! Tell this big, handsome hunk I'm not jailbait."

The good-looking bartender in a wife-beater smiled, gave a thumbs up and yelled, "He's legal."

"There, ya see—I just look young for my age," Chuck said, giggling and running his hand up O.B.'s arm, rubbing his biceps. "Now tell me your real name," he added. "You're just too, too hunky butch to be a Sam. You gotta be a Troy or a Trent or—maybe—an Arnold. Yeah, an Arnold," he said, squeezing the muscle again.

O.B. smiled. "Sam's my real name."

"Oh sure," Chuck countered with a flirtatious smile. "I bet your last name is Smith or Jones. Right?"

"Take your pick," O.B. replied, swallowing a mouthful of his beer.

"Married?"

"Hell no," O.B. said.

"Well, you're hiding something behind that name—Sam." Chuck smiled again and asked, "Are you gonna buy me a drink?"

O.B. nodded. "Sure," he said and signaled for the bartender.

Tim came over and Chuck said, "The usual."

While they waited for Chuck's drink, the young man said, "So, Mr.-Sam-Smith-not-married-Jones, tell me about yourself."

"Nothin' to tell," O.B. said, drinking more of his beer.

"Ah, the strong silent type."

Chuck's drink arrived. He took a sip and tapped a finger to his chin. He said, "Now I'm really curious. What would be so secret that you couldn't give little ol' me a little ol' hint?"

O.B. had no intention of giving Chuck any information. All he wanted from the evening was a good fuck. And the little man's ass was tantalizing enough for the baseball player to ignore the insipid tease talk.

"Why don't you tell me all about you?" O.B. countered.

"Oh, it's a one-way street is it?" Chuck laughed, ran his hand up O.B.'s chest and massaged a nipple through the taut fabric. "Let's just leave both our lives a mystery."

"Fine with me," O.B. said.

They finished their drinks, making small talk as best they could above the pounding music. Since O.B. had a game the next day, he wanted to get to the main event of the evening. He checked his watch. "How about we go somewhere private?"

Chuck pouted again. "I was hopin' you'd ask me to dance first. You're not a wham-bam-thank-you-ma'am kind of man, are you, Sam?"

O.B. rolled his eyes.

"What?" Chuck said, seemingly feigning hurt.

"I don't dance," O.B. lied, wanting to get on with his plan for the evening. He'd wasted enough time with the twink that to start all over could mean going home with nothing but his clenched left fist and lotion to satisfy him. He knew that wouldn't be gratifying.

"Not at all?" Chuck persisted in the same petulant tone.

O.B. shook his head. "Yeah, I dance, but not this fast gyratin' shit."

"Well, we'll just wait for a slow number. Then will you dance with me?"

O.B. sighed, "Yeah, I'll dance with ya. But it better be quick."

"What's your rush, big guy?" Chuck asked, leaning against O.B. "I'm worth waiting for."

O.B. had to agree. The kid had a killer body and for some reason their size differential was really getting to him.

O.B. ordered them another round of drinks as they waited for some music that didn't require hyper-gyrations on the dance floor.

Finally something that could pass for a slow song started. Chuck grabbed O.B.'s hand and dragged him to the floor. O.B. checked his watch. He knew no one would enforce the players' curfew here at home. Still, he had a game the next day and, after just playing a doubleheader, he needed to get proper rest. He would just have to make this a quick whirl around the floor and get on with the main business of the evening.

As the music played, Chuck nestled himself against O.B., reaching up and wrapping his arms around the big man's neck, snuggling his head into the catcher's deep, muscular chest. O.B., in turn, put his arms around the smaller man, stretching down to rub Chuck's firm ass, lightly caressing the man's hair with his lips, thinking of what would be happening in just a short while. O.B. was getting hard quickly as his cock pressed into Chuck's midsection.

Chuck looked up into O.B.'s face and smiled. Then without warning he jumped up and wrapped his legs around O.B.'s waist, laying his head on his partner's shoulder. O.B. cupped the man's ass as Chuck clenched his glutes and rubbed his erection against O.B.'s stomach.

"I want you," Chuck said in a soft, seductive voice as the pair stood and swayed to the music.

"Not as much as I want you," O.B. returned. "Let's get outta here."

O.B. carried his would-be fuck off the dance floor and set him down. He went to the bar, paid their tab and, with an arm around Chuck's shoulder, headed for the door. As they walked out, O.B. caught a glimpse of someone standing at the far end of the bar. His heart skipped a beat. For a moment he thought he recognized the man but didn't know from where. When he looked back again the man was gone.

"How'd ya get here?" O.B. asked once they were out in the parking lot.

"Cab," Chuck replied.

Good, O.B. thought. *Don't have to deal with that "I'll follow you home" shit.*

"Come on," O.B. said as he led Chuck to his Alfa Romeo.

"Ooh, Daddy! Nice wheels," the little man said.

O.B. brushed off the comment, hoping it wouldn't lead to questions about the source of his being able to afford such a car. "Yeah, well—get in. Where do you live?"

"Oh, we can't go to my house," Chuck said, reaching across the console to give the inside of O.B.'s leg a squeeze. "I live with my folks. Can't we go to your place?"

Shit, O.B. thought. He lived in an upscale condo with security cameras all over the fucking place. He'd be seen and recorded bringing a guy home with him.

"Fuck, no," he spat, letting his frustration show.

"You sure you're not married? Usually it's married guys that can't take a date ho—."

"I told you I'm not married!" O.B. said, feeling irritated at his sexual needs being thwarted because he had to stay buried in the closet.

"Okay, okay," Chuck said, withdrawing his hand from O.B.'s thigh.

O.B., sensing the evening might be going south, put his arm around Chuck's shoulders.

"Look, it's complicated. I really want to be with you, but I gotta be careful. We'll go to a motel, all right?"

Chuck seemed to hesitate. "Sure, that's okay," he finally said, searching O.B.'s face as if looking for some clue as to why the man couldn't be more up-front with him.

O.B. had gone the motel route before, although he preferred going to someone's pad. He felt his anonymity was better protected at a private residence. He pulled out of the parking lot and headed across town. He'd go to a Red Roof. They were clean and no one would know him there.

When they got to the motel, he parked away from the office. He couldn't check in himself. They'd ask for ID. He pulled out his wallet and took out a couple of bills and held them out to Chuck.

"You must have some kind of secret," the kid said, taking the money and getting out of the car.

O.B. waited as Chuck went into register for a room. *Damn,* he thought, *being gay and in pro sports is the pits. All this fuckin' sneakin' around and worryin' about bein' caught. Fuck!* O.B. was glad he wasn't into relationships. What could a pro athlete do then? In a relationship you couldn't just stay in bed and fuck. If you had a partner you'd have to divulge more about yourself. You'd have to trust your lover not to talk. But the guy would have friends. He would expect to be able to tell them about you, especially if you were a sports celebrity. And he would want to go out to dinner and stuff. There would be more chance of discovery. No, this one-night, no-strings -attached stuff was the better choice.

He caught sight of Chuck heading back to the car. He let his struggles with the complexities of being a gay sports star recede and turned his mind to the more immediate issue of regenerating the horny mood that had prevailed at the club. *God, this kid is one sexy dude,* O.B. thought as he began to massage his package.

"Room 237," Chuck said, pointing to the far building.

O.B. LAY ON his side. The kid was curled up with his beautiful ass pressed into O.B.'s pubic hair, O.B.'s thick, hard cock between the smaller man's legs, pressing against Chuck's balls. O.B. draped one arm over Chuck's smooth, hairless chest, idly massaging a nip. Chuck moaned softly and wriggled his ass.

Thinking back, the fuck had been exceptional. After a lengthy session of body exploration and mutual sucking, O.B. had eaten the man's ass with relish. As he did, O.B.'s dick throbbed, begging to be buried in the smooth, firm, round, young butt.

When Chuck was ready and open, O.B. rolled on a rubber, applied the lube, and turned the guy over on his back. O.B. pressed the head of his stiff rod against the sphincter. It soon yielded to the pressure and the two became one.

Once inside, O.B. held still to let Chuck adjust to the invasion of his more-than-generous cock. Chuck wrapped his arms around O.B.'s neck, his legs around O.B.'s waist. The big man stood, his hands massaging the globes of Chuck's ass just as they had on the dance floor an hour or so before. He carried Chuck around the room impaled on this throbbing cock, the action causing his prick to push back and forth in the young man's chute and Chuck's hard cock to rub through the dense hair of O.B.'s rippled abs. Chuck moaned, clawed O.B.'s neck, and bit his chest and shoulder.

Much sooner than O.B. wanted, he felt Chuck's cock pulse against him, the warm fluid squirting from it. As Chuck climaxed, he reached up and kissed O.B., his tongue invading the man's mouth just as O.B.'s dick was invading Chuck's ass. O.B. felt his cock stiffen and throb. As the glorious sensations of orgasm flooded his mind and body, O.B. shot his cum into the rubber.

O.B. sat back down on the bed, his cock still buried inside Chuck's body. Chuck reached up and kissed him again.

O.B. lay on his back and slipped from Chuck's hole. Chuck climbed forward, his dick still hard. He wasn't big; maybe five inches. But O.B. took the small, hard cock as well as the balls in his mouth and sucked for all he was worth, enjoying it as if it were a fat, ten-inch tool. Chuck came a second time, O.B. relishing the sweet taste of his cum.

They had showered and now lay together.

O.B. looked over at the clock on the night stand, then kissed the top of Chuck's head. "Time to go," he said, feeling the usual need to be done and on his way.

Chuck pressed his body back against O.B.'s. Though O.B. couldn't see him, the ballplayer could tell by the tone of his voice that Chuck was pouting.

"Why? I want to spend the night with you. I only got you off once. And besides—" Chuck hesitated as if trying to decide if he should continue. "I really like you."

He turned to face O.B.

In the semi-darkness O.B. looked into the young man's face. He was one handsome dude. He was a good fuck, fun to be with, and his small, muscular frame had really been a turn-on. Maybe O.B. could spend the night, just this once.

As quickly as that idea passed through his mind, a second, more compelling, thought came: one of self preservation. *Keep it physical. You're only askin' for trouble if you start encouraging him to feel something more.*

"Sorry, Chucky Boy," O.B. said, forcing his voice into aloofness. "You were a great fuck, but I gotta work tomorrow."

"But tomorrow's Sunday," Chuck protested, reaching down and fondling O.B.'s ample balls and semi-hard dick. Nobody who drives an Alfa works on Sunday. Not unless you're a rock star. Are you a rock star, Sam?"

O.B. winced—not from the pressure on his nuts, but from letting something slip that might give Chuck a clue as to who he might be.

"Look. As much as I'd like to fuck ya again—"

"Or let me suck you off?" Chuck said seductively.

"Or have ya suck me off, I gotta go. Get dressed. I'll get ya a cab."

"When can I see you again?" Chuck asked, getting up from

the bed and beginning to gather his clothes.

"Maybe we'll run into each other at the club," O.B. said, slipping on his briefs. He could see the man was disappointed. He walked over to Chuck, lifted him off the floor, and pulled the smaller guy into a hug. Once again the difference in their size made him feel good. "Look, we had a great time tonight. The sex was great. Let's let it go at that. I'm not into complicated stuff, okay? If we cross paths again—well, then we'll see."

Chuck laid his head on O.B.'s hair-covered chest. "Okay," he said. This time there was no fake poutiness. The boy seemed genuinely sad.

Chapter 2

"BENSON! HEY BENSON!" The voice of Jeff Schneider, the Thunderbolts pitching coach, cut through the fog that swirled in O.B.'s mind. He'd had a rough night. Sleep had come easily but he'd wakened several times from disturbing dreams. Some were about Chuck. In those dreams he'd imagined Chuck as more than a casual fuck, more like someone he cared about. The other dreams, which bothered him the most, were more like nightmares. In them the stranger he had seen at the bar and thought he recognized was stalking him, trying to find out who he was. It seemed to O.B. in the dream that the man wanted to expose him, to let the world and his teammates know he was a gay baseball player. The worst part was toward morning, when he'd woken with a start. He thought he knew who the man was. The guy was someone O.B. had seen before, but couldn't quite put his finger on who or where.

"What?" O.B. barked as he shook off the images he was

mulling over.

"What?" the coach barked back. "Whaddaya mean 'what?' We got a game in two hours and we're supposed to be goin' over their fuckin' battin' roster to plan pitchin' strategies so we can sweep these guys this afternoon. You think you can stop daydreamin' long enough about the cunt you screwed last night to do that?"

The group of pitchers in the clubhouse chuckled as O.B. glared at them. He was tempted to retort something about he was still able to get it up, unlike some others in the room. The pitching coach was an older man and probably well past his prime as a fucker. But O.B. thought better of it since it wasn't any pussy he'd dipped his dick in last night. Instead he just mumbled, "Sorry." For the rest of the session he tried to focus on the details of each of the batters they'd be facing and which pitches would be most effective against them.

As the players were dismissed, the Bolts' manager came in. Whitey Woodson was a legendary baseball man. He'd played on three World Series championship teams, had coached successfully for many years, and had managed a number of teams to pennant championships and two World Series wins. He was tough as nails and respected by his players and the media. You didn't mess with him if he wanted something done. He was a bit under the gun this season as the Bolts weren't doing as well as the fans thought they should be.

"Benson!" the manager called out.

"Yes, sir?" O.B. replied.

"One of the TV stations wants to do some human interest stories on the team. I figured we need some positive publicity this season, so I said yeah. They're sending a reporter over this afternoon."

O.B. nodded, feeling uneasy.

"The guy says the station wants to do players that don't get much attention but play a big part in the team's success. You know, the unsung hero crap," Whitey went on.

O.B. took a deep breath and nodded again.

"So I suggested that he do a story on the catchers. Since you're the startin' catcher, you're on."

Shit! O.B. thought, hoping his distaste for the idea didn't show on his face.

"He wants to meet you after the game today. You got a problem with that?"

O.B. knew very well when Whitey Woodson asked in that manner, your answer had to be, "No sir."

"Good, he'll hook up with you in the locker room. Name's—shit some fruity kinda name—sounds like Emily... uh...Avery; yeah that's it, Avery, Avery Turner. Who the fuck'd name their kid Avery? You can bet how he turned out."

O.B. figured Whitey's homophobia was showing and felt a pang of apprehension.

"Anyway, he's with WQBX."

WQBX was the biggest local TV station. Up to this point O.B. had been successful in maintaining a low profile, keeping his face out of the news by declining interviews and avoiding pictures. He'd been grateful for his catcher's mask. Now came this order from on high that couldn't be ignored.

"Yes, sir," he said obediently.

"Good man," Whitey said, clapping him on the shoulder. "By the way, you're doin' a bang-up job behind the plate, O.B. Now if we could just get the damn pitchers to *find* the plate, we'd be doin' all right." The manager shot an accusative look at Schneider, the pitching coach, who was still in the room talking to a couple of players.

"Thank you, sir," O.B. replied, wishing he could take pride in his manager complimenting him. But instead he felt the anxiety over being interviewed drain the joy from the comment.

"Keep it up," the manager said and walked out of the clubhouse.

THE GAME HAD gone surprisingly well. O.B. had been able to focus on the play despite the distractions of his dreams and the impending interview with Avery Turner. The Thunderbolts had swept the series with the reigning World Champions, winning the final game eight to five.

Great way to go into the fuckin' interview that will probably end my career, O.B. thought sarcastically as he made his way to the locker room.

Once again dodging his way through the mob of players and reporters, he looked around for anyone who might appear to be looking for him. No one seemed to be interested in tracking him down, so he sat on a bench and waited.

Maybe he changed his mind? he thought hopefully, though he knew deep down that was just wishful thinking.

Haskel the sexy trainer walked by. "You gonna stop in for a rubdown?" he asked.

"Naw, Whitey wants me to do a fuckin' interview," O.B. responded. He much preferred the prospect of lying on the training table with Haskel's hands on his body than sitting in front of a camera being grilled by some reporter.

"Okay," the handsome blond said, "but I'll be there if ya want me."

O.B. nodded and tried not to let any ideas of what that statement might imply get to him.

After waiting for about ten minutes he undressed, grabbed a towel, and headed for the showers. There were several players already in the shower room. All were feeling pretty good after sweeping the best team in the league. There was lots of horseplay and teasing. O.B. moved to the far end of the room. He usually joined in a shower-room celebration, but this time he had too much on his mind. He just watched.

Anyone who thinks football players have got the great bodies should visit a major league locker room sometime, he thought, allowing himself to admire his teammates, now freed of their uniforms. The well-hung, muscular hunks pushed, splashed, and punched one another, playing a little grab-ass along the way. O.B. wondered just how far beneath the surface some level of man-to-man attraction might be hidden.

His voyeurism had an effect on his libido and he forgot the upcoming interview. His dick, always on alert, responded to the display of manly interaction and rose to a semi-salute.

When he finished his shower, O.B. made his way through the guys still working on theirs. He took his towel from the hook inside the door and walked into the locker room drying his hair. Without looking up, he made his way to his locker.

"Hi, I'm Avery Turner."

The greeting caught O.B. by surprise and he raised his head to find a handsome young man straddling the bench next to his locker, smiling up at him.

O.B. stood gaping at the man, forgetting that he was naked with his half-hard dick pointing invitingly toward the man's mouth.

"Pleased to meet ya," O.B. mumbled and stuck out his hand. Then, realizing his condition, he added, "Shit," and awkwardly tried to cover his swollen manhood with his towel.

O.B. recognized the reporter. Avery Turner was the man in his dream, the man he'd seen at the Out and Proud, who he'd thought he'd seen before. Avery was also the reporter who'd checked him out Saturday when he'd come out of the shower and, like today, O.B. had had to cover his partially-stiff cock with his towel.

"*Déjà vu*," the reporter said with a wry smile as he stood and took O.B.'s hand.

"I'm sorry," O.B. mumbled self-consciously.

Avery laughed. "Absolutely no problem, O.B.," he said, glancing down at the tented towel. "No problem at all."

Just then another man came up to the pair. "This is Jim," Avery said as the man approached and offered O.B. his hand.

"He's our cameraman. He'll be filming the interview. Jim, Whitey said we could use the conference room in the clubhouse."

Still flustered, O.B. sputtered, "Ya want me to get dressed?" He blushed at the stupidity of his question.

Avery smiled broadly. "Well, personally I'd be fine with you just the way you are. But we'd better go for a more modest look, since this will play on the prime-time news."

Fuck! What the hell! Is the guy fuckin' gay?

O.B. looked at Avery, then at Jim. Neither showed any reaction to Avery's apparent admission that he liked looking at naked men.

Avery matter-of-factly turned to Jim. "You can go set up the equipment. We'll be with you in a few minutes."

Jim left. Apparently Avery had no intention of following and sat where he was, smiling at the big catcher.

"I...uh...I guess I'll get dressed then," O.B. stammered.

"Okay," Avery said, still grinning.

O.B. self-consciously dropped the towel and began dressing. He could feel Avery's eyes on him. As the reporter continued to watch, he went over his plan for the interview. The situation was becoming more and more ludicrous. Here O.B. was, about to be interviewed by a gay man who was apparently not too deep in the closet. When it aired on television the interview would make him recognizable—something he had worked hard to hide for the sake of his secret lifestyle. O.B.'s head was spinning.

O.B. PACED THE floor in his apartment. After the events of the past twenty-four hours he felt like a caged lion. It was bound to happen sooner or later, he thought. *You can't be gay in a high-profile professional sport and expect to live the life you want. Somebody's gonna find out.*

Since the guy who'd done the interview had turned out to

be the man he'd seen in the gay bar the night before, O.B. was wary of going back to the Out and Proud in case Avery would be there. Avery hadn't let on that he'd seen O.B. leaving with Chuck, but O.B. wasn't gonna take a chance.

Although he considered them below his standards, he thought of going to one of the other gay establishments in town. Avery had said the interview wouldn't be aired until midweek. That gave O.B. a couple more nights of anonymity. Once the piece appeared on the evening news, his gay life would be severely curtailed. O.B. had watched the interview with Avery after it had been taped and, while the reporter had said it would be edited, there was no way he wouldn't be recognizable. His days of concealing his face behind his catcher's mask were over.

For the most part, the interview had gone well. Avery asked questions about the catcher's role and its importance to the team. However, it had broken down when O.B. had been pressed for details of his personal life. Avery had stopped the filming a couple of times to encourage O.B. to be more forthcoming. One of the goals of the dialogue was to increase fan awareness of how the players were just regular guys, and just to talk about baseball. O.B. had been vague when asked about his leisure activities. And when asked whether or not he had a girlfriend, O.B. had become flustered to the point that he was sure Avery, if the man had any gaydar at all, would have suspected something.

Maybe I'm gonna have to get a fake girlfriend, O.B. thought. He'd done that on occasion when he'd gone out with the other players. It wasn't hard. There were always a group of women who followed the team around who were all too willing to be seen with ballplayers—and they put out, too. O.B. wouldn't be interested in going that far to cover himself. *Might not be a bad idea, though, if Avery got any vibes of me bein' gay.*

He sat on the couch, covered his face with his hands, and tried to bring some rationality to his thinking. The phone rang, startling him. He leaned over and checked the caller ID—Avery

Turner.

What's he callin' me for? O.B. thought while at the same time feeling a tingle in his groin.

"Hello," he said.

"Hi, O.B., it's Avery."

"Uh…hi…um…how're you doin'? Do we need to do somethin' more with the interview?"

Avery chuckled. "No, it turned out just fine. I'm actually calling to ask you out for a drink."

"A—a drink?"

Avery chuckled again. "Yep, a drink. You do drink, don't you?"

"Yeah, I do. But why?"

"I just thought I'd like to get to know you better. And I also thought maybe you might like to talk about things with someone who'd understand."

"Shock" was the way O.B. would describe his reaction later. He just sat with his mouth open, staring across the room. His brain seemed to have frozen.

Avery continued. "So, what about it? I could meet you about nine at Jason's. That's a pub on Bentley, pretty near your condo."

O.B.'s paranoia kicked in. "How do you know where I live?" he asked suspiciously.

"Relax," Avery said in a soothing voice. "The front office gave me your phone number and address. I told them I needed to do a little more background on you for the interview. So is it a date?"

A date? What do you mean a fuckin' date? What are you, my boyfriend all of a sudden? O.B. felt panic rising and fought to control it.

"Well? How about it?" came Avery's voice again, still composed and relaxed. It had a calming effect on O.B.

"Um. Okay, sure. I'll see you about nine."

"Great, see you then. Bye for now." Avery hung up.

Shit! What am I getting myself into!

After Avery's call he made himself a stiff drink and sat on the couch, considering the man's words. "I just thought I'd like to get to know you better. And I also thought maybe you might like to talk about things with someone who'd understand."

What did Avery mean by that? Is his gaydar sharp enough to have discovered I'm gay?

O.B. decided to shower and shave. He looked at himself in the mirror and thought, *Maybe I'll grow a beard after the fuckin' video comes out. Maybe that'll make me unrecognizable again.* Then he carefully picked out something to wear that would accentuate his plentiful male attributes: deep chest, powerful arms, and slim waist. His pants were just tight enough to show off his fine ass and ample package without being too obvious.

As O.B. dressed he thought about Avery. *He looks like he's got a great body, like he takes care of himself, works out. Not as big as me but that's the way I mostly like 'em anyway. Nice blue eyes, killer smile. Wonder if he's got much body hair? He don't look like he does. How old is he? Probably not much older than me. Couldn't be more than thirty.*

Hell, why am I doing this? he thought. But he made no attempt to stop his meticulous preparations to meet Avery or his musings about the reporter as he applied gel to his mane of dark brown hair.

O.B. WALKED INTO Jason's a little after 9:20. He looked around the pub. He didn't see Avery at first. He checked his watch and scolded himself for purposely coming a bit late, so as not to look to anxious. Maybe Avery'd gotten tired of waiting, decided O.B. wasn't going to show and left. Finally, however, O.B. located him at the bar. His relief that he hadn't missed Avery surprised him but it was quickly replaced by anxiety when he saw the man at the bar talking with a tall, good-looking guy.

O.B. didn't know what to do. Since he was in a quandary about meeting Avery in the first place, his initial instinct was to just duck out. However, as he stood and decided his next move, Avery saw him and waved him over. O.B. took a deep breath and headed in Avery's direction.

When O.B. came up to the two men, Avery extended a hand and said, "Glad you could make it." Then turning to the stranger next to him said, "O.B. this is Jason Smallish, the owner of the pub and a good friend of mine. Well actually he's more than a friend. Jason's my ex."

The two men nodded at each other. O.B. smiled weakly and shifted his weight uncomfortably.

Avery continued with the introductions. "Jason, this is O.B. Benson. He's the catcher for the Thunderbolts I told you about. I did the interview with him today."

Just how much more did you tell him? O.B. thought, his discomfort at the situation increasing.

O.B. took the hand Jason offered him and the two men exchanged greetings. Jason wasn't in the least represented by his surname. He wasn't anywhere near smallish. Tall and nicely built, Jason could have easily been a target for an evening of fun if this had been the Out and Proud instead of a straight establishment.

Once the introductions had been completed, Jason excused himself.

Avery smiled at O.B. It was a smile that made O.B.'s cock sit up and take notice. He tried to ignore his prick's reaction and smiled back.

"Can I get you a drink?"

O.B. had had two drinks at home to get him ready for the meeting. Since he didn't have a game the next day he threw caution to the wind and said, "Scotch, Black Label, on the rocks."

Avery signaled the bartender and ordered. When the drinks arrived the men carried them to a table a little apart. As they sat, O.B. studied the handsome Avery in the glow of the candle on the table. He wondered if the man had chosen this out-of-the-way location on purpose so they could talk more freely.

"Thanks for the drink," O.B. said, raising his glass to his host.

"My pleasure," Avery responded.

O.B. didn't know what to say next. He sat there looking around the well-appointed room. He glanced at Avery, who sat with his arms folded across his chest, smiling at him.

"Um, nice place," O.B. eventually offered. "I've never been here before, even though it's pretty close to my—"

"It's not easy being gay in the major leagues, is it?" Avery interrupted in a tone that was so genuine and sincere it almost made O.B. want to immediately open up to the man.

His years of practiced denial of his sexual orientation kicked in. "What the fuck are you talkin' about? Who're you callin' a limp-wristed gay?"

Avery smiled and took a deep breath. "Pro athletes see themselves as machismo personified, don't they? And a typical macho man has to hide his own sexuality by expressing the view of homosexuals as weak, sissy-boys. Despite the changing views of our society, pro sports is still home for homophobes. So relax, Mr. Benson. I'm not about to out you. I know what that'd do to your career."

"'Out' me? What makes you think I'm afraid of being outed? I mean—" O.B. blustered, panicking again. "I'm not gay. I don't have any reason to be outed."

"Relax. It's okay. I'm gay and when I came out it wasn't the end of the world. I thought that if I did I'd be banned from the locker rooms. But I'm not. There're still guys who are nervous that I'm going to jump them, but for the most part it didn't change anything for me."

O.B. glared at Avery.

The reporter continued. "I know it's not the same for you. There are no openly gay men in any major sport in the U.S. There's a strict code of silence. I'm not here to try to convince you to be the first."

Deciding Avery had his number, O.B. gave up trying to deny it and said, "Yeah, well what the fuck do you think that interview's gonna do? I worked damn hard to keep myself outta the news and now, once that fuckin' thing goes on air, everyone'll know my face and I won't be able to—"

"I'm sorry," Avery said, sincerity clearly showing in his voice. "That's why I wanted to meet with you tonight, to assure you I didn't choose you for the interview. That was Whitey's doing."

"No, well maybe you didn't pick me, but the interview was your idea."

Avery's sexy smile permeated the air once more, making O.B. feel warm and less defensive.

"Wrong again. The assignment was given to me by the team and the station brass. I had nothing to do with it other than to agree to do the interviews."

O.B. understood. He was attacking the messenger. He bent his head, took a breath and tried to relax. When he felt he had himself under control he looked at Avery and said, "How did you know I was gay?"

"I actually didn't," Avery said, taking a sip of his drink. "Not for sure anyway. There were a couple of things that made me think you might be—mainly how flustered you got when I pushed you about your personal life. But it was mostly wishful thinking. There's nothing in your manner or looks that would tip anyone off if that's what you're worried about. You're well under anyone's gaydar." He smiled that cock-teasing smile again.

"Fuck!" O.B. whispered, realizing it was his own paranoia that had led him to give Avery reason to suspect him and then to trick him into outing himself. But now that it was in the open between them, he felt more comfortable, even glad at the turn of events.

"You're the first person who I ever admitted to bein' gay and a baseball player in the same breath. Where do we go from here?" O.B. asked.

"My place," Avery replied. "If you're interested. I take it you'd rather not take me home to mother just yet."

O.B.'s surprise at the answer must have shown on his face because Avery laughed.

"Didn't expect that, did you?"

"Well, no. I guess I shoulda said where do *I* go from here now that my cover is gonna be blown."

"Well, if you'd rather not come home with me, it's okay."

"No, no, I'm all for it," O.B. said, a huge smile breaking across his ruggedly-handsome face. He allowed, for the first time, the attraction he'd felt for Avery from the moment they'd met, to bloom. "Your place would be just fine."

"NICE DIGS," O.B. commented as he followed Avery into his well-appointed apartment.

"Thanks."

O.B. felt something brush against his leg. He looked down to find a white cat with large orange-and-black spots rubbing its face on his pants and purring loudly.

Avery laughed. "That's Coco," he said in a voice that denoted surprise. "She doesn't usually take to strangers. You must be a real cat lover." Avery bent over and picked the cat up and placed it on his right shoulder where it regarded O.B. through half-closed yellow eyes.

"Uh...I..." O.B. stammered. The truth was, he didn't much care for animals in general. Not that he had anything against them, but he had never had much experience with pets growing up. However, he didn't want to say anything that might put Avery off, so he tentatively reached out to scratch the feline's head and lied, "Yep, cats are pretty cool."

Coco responded by butting O.B.'s hand with her head, completely closing her eyes, her purr engine going into high gear.

"Well, this is pretty amazing," Avery remarked. "I've never seen her take to anyone this way before. Usually if I have someone over she disappears into the closet and isn't seen until she thinks the coast is clear."

The men stood while O.B. continued to stroke Coco and she, in turn, continued to purr. Avery smiled. It was clear to

O.B. that the cat's acceptance of him had made an impression on the reporter. Maybe it was a good omen and O.B. would be getting lucky very shortly.

Avery let the cat drop lightly to the floor. "Would you like a drink?"

O.B. wasn't used to this, first the pet and now the offer of a drink. His sexual encounters were nearly always pick-ups where the participants had gotten down to business as soon as they arrived at the motel room or the guy's pad. He was already half-hard and ready for action.

"Uh, sure," he said, somewhat perplexed at the unfolding situation.

"What can I get for you? I have a full bar. I can make you just about anything you'd like."

"I'll have whatever you're having."

"You had scotch, Black Label, on the rocks at Jason's. That still okay?"

"Fine," O.B. replied.

Avery fixed drinks for the both of them and turned on some music.

"I'd light the fireplace, but it's a little useless since I've got the AC on," Avery said with a chuckle. He did light a couple of candles on the mantel and lowered the lights.

The romantic approach to an evening together with a man had O.B. off -balance.

The men sat on the couch.

"Here's to the start of an interesting friendship," Avery said, lifting his glass.

O.B. nodded and followed suit.

After they'd sipped their drinks, O.B. wasn't sure what to do. He'd assumed Avery had invited him home for sex. Now it seemed it was to be just an evening of drinks and conversation. Coco had returned and was nestled between the men, her purr motor running.

When some minutes had passed, during which Avery seemed

content to just sit, scratch Coco's ears, and enjoy the moment, O.B. said awkwardly, "What made ya decide to come out?"

Avery glanced thoughtfully at the candles flickering on the fireplace before facing O.B. "I got tired of living a lie."

O.B. felt Avery's statement was a judgment of him and his need to keep his identity hidden.

It must have shown on his face, because Avery quickly added, "Look, I understand your situation. I really do. I know not everyone has a real choice in this, not one that doesn't come with consequences, anyway, but coming out was the right thing to do in my case."

O.B. took another swallow of his drink. "Go on."

"I was married. She was my college sweetheart, a cheerleader. I was the dashing quarterback, captain of the football team, the perfect storybook scenario. Except that I was in love with the star running back." He paused as if remembering.

"Did he know you loved him?" O.B. asked.

"Oh, yes," Avery nodded. "We were roommates and had a great time together. No one suspected what our true relationship was. We hid it well. We even double dated. But we really loved each other."

"Then why did ya get married? Why didn't ya just stick with this guy?" O.B. was getting genuinely interested in Avery's story.

"The same reason you keep yourself buried in the closet; to protect my image, and his. I knew I wasn't going to be big enough to play pro football. I decided to be a sports journalist instead. I didn't think I'd have a chance in hell even as a sports writer if I was out. So I married to hide the truth from the world—and me."

"What about your—uh, your boyfriend?"

"He got married, too. We even went so far as to be best man in each others' weddings. He plays in the NFL now. Everything neatly hidden and covered up by a bunch of lies."

"But you're not married now? Are you?"

"No, after a few years it became clear that it wasn't working for me. Kathy, that was my wife's name, suspected something was wrong because it became more difficult for me to have sex with her. I never cheated on her physically but it was getting harder and harder not to. The only way I could manage to have sex with her was to conjure up some fantasy of a hot ballplayer I'd seen in the locker room. We grew further and further apart. So she started pushing to have kids. I guess she figured if we had kids it would fix what was wrong between us. And I knew that once we had children I couldn't just up and leave. But I also knew that the need to be with a man was getting close to making me do something I'd regret. I know some gay men can be married and have something on the side, but I'm not made that way. Once I make a commitment, it's a commitment."

O.B. drained the last of his scotch.

"Another drink?" Avery asked, getting up and holding out his hand for O.B.'s glass.

O.B. nodded and handed it to him. Coco stood, stretched, and climbed onto O.B.'s lap and lay down. O.B. idly petted the cat as he watched Avery walk away. He took a deep breath, enjoying the man's tight ass, still hoping it would be included in the evening's activities.

"Do you ever see your friend, the football player?" O.B. asked when Avery returned with the drinks.

"Yes, we stay in touch and go out to dinner when he's playing in town. That's about the extent of our relationship."

"You never—?" O.B. asked, not completely believing Avery.

"No. I couldn't do it when I was married and I can't do it with a married man now that I'm not. We're just good friends. I think he'd be willing if I was, but we don't go there."

O.B. was beginning to realize that sex with Avery might not on the agenda. Just to make sure, he asked, "So you don't mess around with anyone unless it's a serious thing?"

"I didn't say that." Avery set his drink on the coffee table and moved closer to O.B. "I mess around lots. But if it becomes serious then I expect the relationship to be respected."

O.B. placed his glass next to Avery's and slipped nearer to the man. Coco jumped off O.B.'s lap and onto the floor with a soft mew of protest.

"Are there any serious relationships goin' on in your life right now?" O.B. asked, putting a hand on Avery's shoulder and massaging it lightly.

"Hmmm, not any that I can think of," the reporter responded, running his tongue across his lips and smiling.

"Good," O.B. said, putting both arms around Avery and pulling him into a kiss.

The kiss blew O.B.'s mind. It was so different from any he could remember. There was passion and a growing sense of arousal, but there was also tenderness and a yearning for something he couldn't quite put his finger on. O.B. broke the kiss and looked deeply into Avery's eyes. The man smiled, put a hand behind O.B.'s head, and pulled him to his lips, his tongue softly but firmly caressing O.B.'s.

O.B. responded, wrapping his powerful arms around the man's waist. He lay back against the sofa cushions, pulling Avery on top of him. He could feel Avery's hard cock pressing against his as they slowly ground their hips against each other.

O.B. ran his hands up and down Avery's back as they shared kisses and caresses. He reached down and massaged Avery's solid, full ass as Avery responded by clenching and relaxing his glutes. O.B. pulled Avery's shirt from his pants and slipped his hands underneath, feeling the warm, smooth flesh of the man's back. Avery pushed himself up to tug O.B.'s shirt free, exposing his taut, muscular torso. Avery ran his fingers through the tangle of thick, almost-black hair until he found O.B.'s sensitive nipples. He lowered his head to kiss and lick them.

O.B. moaned. Avery bit. O.B. moaned louder, flexing his muscular pecs. Avery bit harder. O.B. arched his back as the stimulation of his nips increased his arousal.

"Oh fuck!" O.B. groaned. "Shit."

Avery stood and held out his hand. O.B. took it and got to

his feet. They kissed, O.B. pressing their bodies together in a bone-crushing hug that he hoped would convey his urgent need to make himself one with this man. They broke the kiss and Avery led the way into the bedroom.

Avery left O.B. standing by the bed and went to the nightstand. He took out lube and condoms and laid them on the pillow before walking back to pull O.B.'s shirt all the way off. As O.B. kicked off his shoes, Avery undid the man's belt and pushed his pants and briefs to the floor. O.B. stepped out of them and stripped off his socks. He stood naked. Avery surveyed O.B.'s body with delight in his eyes.

Avery sat on the bed and pulled O.B. toward him, running his hands over O.B.'s ass. He laid his head against O.B.'s rippled, hair-shrouded stomach and nuzzled the thick thatch of pubes, the man's stiff dick rubbing against Avery's neck.

O.B. gasped as Avery turned and swallowed him to the base of his thick cock while gently kneading his bull-sized balls. He could hear Avery's ragged, passionate breathing as the man sucked.

To keep himself from cumming long before he wanted to, O.B. pulled Avery up and kissed him. O.B. removed Avery's shirt as Avery slipped out of his shoes and stripped off his pants and underwear. Still holding the now-naked man, O.B. lowered him to the bed and stretched out full length on top of him, grasping his wrists and pinning him to the mattress.

"You are one beautiful man," O.B. whispered as he slid his body down Avery's smooth, well-defined torso, stopping to briefly engulf the man's rigid organ before continuing down to a pair of sturdy legs.

O.B. knelt on the floor and took off each of Avery's socks, laving and kissing each of the man's feet, sucking his toes.

Still kneeling, O.B. raised Avery's legs and pulled him to the edge of the bed. He began to stroke and kiss Avery's ass, forcing his tongue into the tight crevice between the mounds of muscle until he found Avery's taut hole. He manipulated it with his tongue and fingers, relishing the feel, taste, and slightly musky man-scent. He lifted Avery further and, draping Avery's legs over his shoulders, rubbed his hairy chest against the man's smooth, firm ass.

O.B. stood. Lowering Avery's legs to his waist, he leaned forward and braced himself on his arms. He looked down at the smiling man. Returning the smile, he bent and they kissed. Avery put his arms around O.B.'s neck. O.B. reached down and took his rock-hard cock and ran it up and down Avery's crack. He could feel the pre-cum making it slippery. He found the entry and gave a gentle push. He knew he could enter easily. But he held his position. He looked into Avery's eyes.

"I'd like that, too," Avery said. "But—" he reached over, picked up the condom and lube and held them out to O.B.

O.B. took them, stood, and ripped open the foil. He rolled the rubber into place and slicked Avery with lube. Pressing a finger into the puckered hole elicited a moan from Avery. Repositioning himself, O.B. pressed and slowly entered.

Avery gasped. Wrapping his arms and legs around O.B., he murmured, "Oh, yes. Yes, O.B. Yes."

Holding Avery against him, O.B. initiated a slow rhythm. More mindful of his partner's pleasure than he ever could remember himself being, he timed his thrusts and their depth to elicit the most intense reactions from Avery, trying to discover just what gave the man the greatest enjoyment. To his surprise, he discovered that the more he tried to please Avery, the more satisfaction he derived.

After a much longer time than usual, O.B. felt he had reached the point at which he couldn't hold out any longer. With a groan that was almost a sob, he shot his load. Trembling with post-climactic pleasure, O.B. picked Avery up and carried him farther up on the bed and laid him down. Spooning behind him, O.B. re- entered Avery, reached around and stroked his stiff cock and caressed the back of his neck with kisses. Avery moaned softly and nestled himself back against O.B.'s chest.

A minute or so later, Avery's body stiffened. "O.B.!" he said as came, coating O.B.'s hand in hot cum.

O.B. couldn't tell how long they lay there. Finally he felt himself slip out of Avery's ass. He got up, made his way to the bathroom, disposed of the rubber, and took a piss.

Coming back to bed, he said, "I'd like to stay the night if you'll let me."

"I was hoping you would," Avery said, opening his arms.

O.B. wrapped Avery in a hug. The man's head resting on O.B.'s chest, they fell asleep.

O.B. SLOWLY OPENED his eyes. He felt disoriented. Then he remembered he wasn't at home.

"Hm," he mumbled. *I'm at Avery's.* The thought made him happy. He turned over and reached for the man. The bed next to him was empty.

He sat up. Coco was curled up at the foot of the bed. She raised her head, got up, and stretched a long, leisurely cat stretch. She then jumped lightly to the floor and walked out the door, her tail held high, the tip twitching. O.B. smiled, got up, and went to the bathroom to relieve himself. He slipped on his briefs and wandered out of the bedroom.

The apartment was quiet. He made his way into the kitchen and looked around. There was a note on the table.

O.B.,

Sorry I had to get up and run. You were sleeping so peacefully I didn't have the heart to wake you. Besides, if I did we'd probably find a reason for me to be late for work. LOL. I have a broadcast at eight. If you're up in time you can catch it. Channel 5.

O.B. checked the clock on the stove: 7:35.

There are pancakes and sausage on a plate in the fridge if you don't mind nuking them, the note continued. *OJ is in there, too. Syrup and butter on the table. Coffee on the counter. Towel and soap out for you in the bathroom.*

Thanks for last night. Talk to you soon.

A.

P.S. Coco will probably try to convince you she's starving. Ignore her. She's already had her breakfast.

O.B. looked down and, sure enough, the cat was sitting in front of her bowl, looking up at him with pleading eyes. She meowed plaintively.

"Sorry, cat. Ain't gonna work. I been warned."

She paid no attention to his remark and meowed again.

O.B. smiled. *So this is how the other half lives,* he thought.

O.B. went to the bathroom and showered. As he stood in the warm spray he thought of the night with Avery, comparing it to the one with Chuck. Saturday with Chuck had been all about sex. Sunday with Avery had been something more. He sighed. Saturday was the norm. Sunday, as nice as it was, wasn't going to last.

Subdued by that thought, he stepped out of the shower, dressed, and went to the kitchen.

O.B. switched on the counter TV as he warmed the breakfast Avery had made for him. He sat down at the table and ate. Coco came and sat next to his chair, blinking and looking at him expectantly.

"I don't think I'm supposed to give ya anything."

Coco mewed, shifted her weight back and forth on her front paws, and cocked her head sideways.

"Well, just this once." O.B. dropped a bit of sausage next to the cat. "But don't tell Avery, okay?"

Coco sniffed the morsel, then picked it up and walked away.

"What, no thank you?" O.B. said with a chuckle.

The voice from the television diverted his attention.

"Welcome to the eight o'clock hour of your morning news with Ted and Sally at the news desk, Brandon with the weather, Karla with traffic, and Avery with sports."

As each of the newscast members was introduced their pictures appeared. O.B. smiled when Avery's face flashed on the screen.

"There's your daddy," O.B. called to Coco and pointed to the screen. The cat seemed unimpressed.

About ten minutes later, as O.B. sipped his second cup of coffee, Avery was introduced. Again O.B. smiled as his bed partner from the previous night detailed the Thunderbolts' most recent win. Then the scene shifted and Avery was sitting at the news desk with the anchors. He was introducing the series of interviews he'd be doing with players from the Bolts.

"The first interview will be with O.B. Benson, the starting catcher," Avery said. As he continued telling viewers that it would air on the prime time news Wednesday night, a clip of the taped interview played. O.B. let out a deep sigh as he saw himself talking with Avery.

"Good-bye, cover," he said, shaking his head.

Chapter 3

ON HIS WAY back to his condo from Avery's, O.B. stopped at the supermarket to pick up a few things. When he got to the checkout lane a young man walking by called out, "Hey, O.B.!" and gave him the thumbs up. O.B., with a tinge of apprehension, gave the kid a weak smile.

The man standing in line behind O.B. turned around, a look of recognition crossing his face. "You're O.B. Benson, aren't you?" The man took O.B.'s hand to shake it before it had even been offered. "I saw you on the news this morning. How're you guys gonna do against the Rays? You did real well in the last series. Maybe this is the turnaround, you think?" O.B.'s anxiety increased.

O.B. told him he thought they'd do well against the Rays and went on with the business of putting his purchases on the conveyor belt. The clerk at the register smiled, then turned to the woman at the next register and said loudly, "Maggie, this here is O.B. Benson. You know, that baseball player that was on the news this morning. Ain't he a hunk?"

By now O.B. was thoroughly embarrassed and ready to crawl in a hole. In all his years with the Thunderbolts he'd never once been recognized in public. Now suddenly everyone seemed to know him and it had only been a quick trailer on the morning news. What would it be like once they played the full interview?

By the time O.B. made it to his car, he'd been asked for his autograph three times. If it hadn't been for the night he'd just spent with Avery, he'd be ready to strangle the reporter. He'd hoped to get to the Out and Proud at least once before the interview aired on Wednesday, but his new celebrity meant his solitary confinement would have to start immediately.

As he walked into his apartment, the phone was ringing. "Avery," he said aloud as he checked the caller ID. He sighed as feelings of both depression and joy filled him.

Settling himself on the couch, he pressed the answer button. "Hi," he said.

"Hi," Avery returned. "Just calling to see if you did all right this morning?"

"Yeah, fine, thanks," O.B. answered.

"Was that breakfast enough for you?"

"Yeah, sure. It was great," O.B. answered again.

Avery was silent for a few seconds before saying, "Is something wrong?"

Realizing blaming Avery for fate intervening in his life was stupid, O.B. said, "I'm sorry. Nothing to do with you. Well, yeah, maybe it kinda is." He laughed ruefully. "But I sorta got recognized a buncha times at the store on the way home."

"I'm sorry."

O.B. could tell from Avery's tone that he truly felt bad.

"Guess I'll have to confine my sexual escapades to your apartment," O.B. said with a rueful laugh.

"Would that be all that bad? I thought we hit it off pretty well last night."

O.B. wasn't sure how to answer. He didn't know if Avery was being serious or not. He also wasn't sure how he felt about a second go-around. Yeah, Avery was a good fuck, a nice guy, really sexy, handsome, but—*but what? You can't go cruisin' anymore. Not with your face out there.*

"If I didn't know better, I'd say you planned this," O.B. said, keeping his voice light.

Avery laughed. "Yes. It was my devious plot from the first time I laid my eyes on that awesome body of yours."

Still not quite sure whether Avery was kidding, O.B. laughed with him.

"I guess I'm your default boyfriend then," O.B. said.

"Come over for dinner. I'll grab a couple of steaks on the way home."

O.B. hesitated. Two nights in a row was unusual for him. Then he said, "Okay, can I bring anything?"

"No use both of us going shopping. Besides, you don't want to get mobbed again, do you?" Avery replied, laughing softly. "Anything special you want to drink? Or for dessert?"

"Nope. Whatever you think of will be good. But I feel like I should bring something."

Avery insisted, "Just bring your appetite and that sexy bod of yours. That's all I need."

O.B. smiled. "Okay. See ya later," he said, feeling a happy anticipation.

O.B. LAY SPOONED against a sleeping Avery.

The evening had been great. Avery was a good chef. The steaks, salad, and baked potato were just the way O.B. liked them. He'd helped Avery with the dishes, then they'd sat on the couch drinking wine and talking for several hours. They'd made out and then retired to the bedroom, where the sex had been spectacular. Afterward they'd showered together.

O.B. softly stroked Avery's hair and thought about how different this was from anything he'd ever even imagined he would get involved in. He'd always dismissed any unwelcome, stray idea of sex in the context of a relationship with a man. Sex that expressed any emotion other than lust was foreign to him. Yet here he was, spending his second night with this man, feeling— he wasn't sure what label to use. He was happy, happier than he had been in a long time. He was content, satisfied, not the usual emptiness he experienced when he picked someone up, fucked their brains out, and went home to a lonely apartment. But *happy, content, satisfied* weren't the complete description of how he felt just then, lying there, holding Avery close.

He liked Avery. He liked the man's sexy body, handsome face, and wonderful smile. But he also liked the things Avery said, how the guy made him laugh and feel relaxed and comfortable in his sexuality. O.B. liked feeling free to be able to experience these emotions. He sensed something inside of him was changing, but he wasn't sure how to deal with it. His eyes began to close.

The next thing O.B. was aware of was the side of his face being licked and a loud purring in his ear—Coco. During the night he and Avery must have turned over. Now Avery was spooned against him, his arm draped across O.B.'s chest. Avery nuzzled the back of his neck.

The licking and purring persisted, interspersed with insistent meows.

"Uh, Avery? Should we do something about this?" O.B. asked.

Avery stirred, raised his head, saw Coco, then laughed. "Looks like you're the chosen one. She wants her breakfast," he said, rolling away from O.B. and starting to climb out of bed. Coco stopped her licking, jumped to the floor, and pranced out of the bedroom.

"Do you want me to get it for her?" O.B found himself asking as if it were the most natural thing in the world for him to do.

"Thanks, no. You're my guest." Avery said leaning over and

kissing O.B. on the nose. "I'll feed her, or she'll just pester us until I do. Be right back." He followed Coco out of the bedroom.

O.B. got up and used the bathroom, then lay back down. In a few minutes Avery got back in bed, snuggling tightly against the big man's body once more.

"Does she do that every mornin'?" O.B. asked, pulling Avery closer.

"Yes. Coco's better than an alarm clock. Haven't overslept since I got her. But we don't have to get up just yet."

O.B. smiled, kissed Avery's head, and gave him a squeeze.

After about fifteen minutes of dozing, O.B. felt Avery stirring. He opened his eyes to find Avery smiling at him.

"Good morning again," Avery said before pulling O.B. into a prolonged kiss.

O.B. could feel himself getting hard.

Avery must have been able to feel O.B.'s response, because he said, "We've got time."

O.B. didn't need encouragement. He wrapped his arms around Avery and rolled over until he was on top. He ground his blooming erection against Avery's.

"I'm gonna fuck you," O.B. said with a grin, pinning Avery's wrists over his head.

"I was hoping you'd say that," Avery replied, squirming under the weight of the ballplayer's body.

O.B. leaned down and kissed Avery, pressing their chests together. Letting his legs straddle Avery's, he ground his dick against Avery's abs as the two men deepened the kiss.

O.B. rolled off Avery, reached into the drawer of the nightstand, and pulled out a condom and lube. "Turn on your side," he instructed.

Avery did as he was told. O.B. shifted so he lay with his chest against Avery's back, a leg draped over Avery's chest, and his face against Avery's ass. He loved Avery's butt, so firm and smooth. He'd never enjoyed eating someone out as much as he did Avery. O.B. leaned in and kissed the firm cheeks, running his tongue up and down the crevice before spreading the muscular mounds and seeking out the pink, puckered hole with his tongue.

Avery moaned with pleasure as O.B. worked first a tongue, then a finger into his ass, loosening him.

Changing position again, O.B. scooted up against Avery's back, pressed his cock against the now open hole and slid easily inside. He lay there for a moment, relishing the feeling of being joined together.

Avery twisted his head and they exchanged hungry kisses.

Slowly, O.B. began a rhythmic thrusting. He ran his hands over Avery's chest, rubbing the erect nips before seeking out Avery's cock and balls. He massaged them as he buried his face in Avery's neck. O.B. relished the building sensations of sexual arousal. As he felt himself approaching climax, he concentrated his attention on Avery's throbbing dick. He wanted them to cum together.

"Let me know when you're gonna shoot," O.B. commanded.

Avery grunted his assent.

The intoxicating emotions of the culmination of their union increased and O.B. felt a tingling in the small of his back as he came close to his peak. He held back, waiting for Avery.

Avery moaned, "Now!" and clenched his ass muscles around O.B.'s cock.

As O.B. felt Avery's dick throb in his hand and saw the warm fluid spurt from its head, he let himself go and could feel his cum gush into the rubber that separated his cock from Avery's body. In the midst of his climax, the barrier caused him a moment of regret. He didn't want to be separated from Avery, even by a thin layer of latex. The thought bewildered him, but he forced it aside and allowed only feelings of intense sexual pleasure to permeate the moment.

They lay there, letting their breathing and heart rates return to normal. O.B. kissed the back of Avery's neck and pulled him close. He wanted to turn aside his rising emotions. He tried to call up the feelings that were more familiar to him after sex—

aloofness and detachment. But he couldn't. O.B. had to admit he had feelings for Avery that evoked both joy and anxiety.

He was relieved when Avery broke into his thoughts and said, "Let's shower and we'll get breakfast. I have to get to the studio."

O.B. held Avery tight and kissed him one more time. Breaking the kiss, he looked into Avery's eyes.

"What?" Avery asked, smiling back at him.

O.B. took a deep breath. "Nothing. I have to get going, too. Got a game today."

"Yep, I know," Avery said with a chuckle. "I'll be covering the game, you know?" He gave O.B. another peck, got out of bed, and walked to the bathroom. "I'll be interviewing Neil Carter as part of the TV series today after the game."

As he disappeared through the door, two reactions hit O.B. Avery would be at the ball field. How would they behave toward each other after the two nights they'd just spent together? As that thought faded it was replaced with a surge of emotion that, if O.B. didn't know better, bordered on jealousy.

Neil Carter, huh? You better not be inviting him home for dinner!

He realized how stupid that thought was. He had no right to limit Avery's sex life. O.B. got out of bed to join Avery in the shower.

THE GAME HADN'T gone well. O.B. couldn't concentrate during the pre-game strategy meeting. He'd kept having thoughts about the last two nights with Avery, the upcoming airing of his interview, the fact that he would be seeing Avery in the locker room after the game, and, most annoying of all, and much to O.B.'s surprise, the interview Avery would be doing with Neil. As a consequence, he'd misread a couple of batters, given the pitcher the wrong signals, and it had cost the Thunderbolts a couple of runs. They had won the game but O.B. came off the field and into the locker room disgruntled and frustrated, blaming himself for the near loss.

Fuck, I wouldn't have been thinkin' any of that shit if it weren't for the stupid interview. I'd be concentratin' on my job and on goin' out and findin' some anonymous ass to screw instead of worryin' about bein' recognized and what's goin' on in my head with Avery.

He threw his protective catcher's gear at the equipment manager, who responded with an appropriate epithet, which elicited a "Fuck you!" from O.B. He then stomped to his locker, tossed his mitt inside, slammed the door, and gave it a kick.

Just then Haskel, the trainer, came down the aisle between the rows of lockers.

"Hey, looks like somebody needs a few kinks worked out. What's goin' on, man? Need a little time on the table to help you relax, O.B.?"

O.B. looked at him. The sight of the handsome trainer did little to unravel the confusion in his mind about his situation with Avery. He knew a rubdown and work on his legs would be good for him, but in his current state of mind he didn't know if he could handle it, especially from a hot, sexy man like Haskel. *Wouldn't be fair to Avery.*

That thought was immediately followed by, *What the hell! Wouldn't be fair to Avery? What's goin' on, Benson? You're fuckin' losing it! What does Avery have to do with my gettin' it off with a rubdown?*

"Shit!" O.B. said aloud, startling Haskel.

"Hey man, what's wrong? You okay?" he said.

"Just upset about the way I'm playin'," the catcher said. There was no way he was going to reveal the reasons behind his poor performance to anyone.

"Well, come on into the training room after your shower, and we'll fix you up," said.

O.B. nodded. "Yeah, okay, I'll think about it." he added unenthusiastically.

Haskel gave him a pat on the shoulder and walked off down the aisle toward the training room. O.B. sat down on the bench with his head in his hands. *No way I'm goin' to the fuckin' trainin' room—not today!*

"Benson."

O.B. looked up. It was Neil Carter. O.B. felt his irritation flare again.

"Hey," the right fielder said. "You did an interview with this guy Turner from the TV station, right?"

"Yeah, what about it?"

"I hear he's a fag."

O.B. felt his irritation turn to anger.

"Did he put the make on you or try anything?" Neil continued.

Images of the past couple of days with Avery flashed through O.B.'s mind. His anger changed to fear. He struggled to keep control. Standing and turning away from Neil, he pretended to rearrange things in his locker.

"Naw, he didn't try nothin'. We just did the interview and that was it. But he better keep his hands off me," Neil went on. "Don't know why they let fuckin' queers in the locker room. Makes me nervous."

O.B. turned to face Neil once again. He felt caught between a desire to defend Avery and a need to protect himself. As O.B. opened his mouth to say something, Avery rounded the corner of the row of lockers and came up behind Neil.

"Gentlemen," Avery said with a smile that O.B. felt was directed especially to him.

Neil spun around to face the newcomer.

"Hello, O.B. Nice to see you again," Avery said casually, sticking out his hand for O.B. to shake.

O.B. took Avery's hand and felt a mixture of thrill and apprehension.

"Neil," Avery continued, directing his attention to the right fielder. "I'm Avery Turner, WQBX TV. I'll be doing the interview with you today."

Neil hesitated for a second, glanced at O.B., but finally

reached out and took Avery's offered hand.

Homophobic bastard! O.B. thought.

"I'll wait while you take your shower. We'll be in the conference room in the clubhouse. I'll meet you there when you're ready, and we'll go over the format for the piece," Avery said with a smile.

O.B. was relieved on some level that Avery hadn't wanted to ambush Neil by waiting for him by his locker as he came out of the shower like had happened before O.B.'s interview. At the same time, O.B. was rattled by Neil's comments about Avery.

When Neil left, O.B. stood awkwardly by his locker, feeling embarrassed to take his clothes off in front of Avery, despite having been intimate with the man for the past couple of days.

Avery leaned against the wall of lockers. "Neil seems a bit nervous."

"Yeah, well, I was, too, if you remember."

Avery chuckled. "You still look a little unnerved. What's wrong?"

O.B. looked around uncomfortably.

"Oh, I get it," Avery said. "Look, there's not going to be a big scarlet 'GAY' on your chest when you take off your shirt."

"Avery, for God's sake!" O.B. said in an undertone.

"It's okay," Avery said in his calm, reassuring voice. "Believe me, no one's going to know we've been together."

O.B. sighed.

"How about dinner again tonight? We could go to Jason's." Avery said.

O.B. hesitated. After what Neil had said, maybe seeing Avery in public wasn't such a good idea. Being seen with him there once might be explained away, but twice?

Avery must have sensed his ambivalence.

"Or we could do dinner again at my place?"

O.B.'s first instinct was to refuse. He didn't know where this was going. He'd never been with a man two nights in a row, let alone three. Yet something inside of him was making a stronger case for saying yes.

"Sure, yeah, okay."

Seven o'clock all right with you?"

O.B. nodded.

"Great."

Avery leaned closer. "O.B., the surest way to make people suspicious is to be uptight. Relax. No one's going to guess we're seeing each other." He reached out and squeezed O.B.'s shoulder.

O.B. smiled, somewhat reassured. But he glanced around anyway, just to make sure no one had seen the exchange.

"See you at seven," Avery said and walked away.

O.B. watched Avery go. He shook his head and pulled off his jersey. He glanced down at his chest. Sure enough, there was no scarlet 'GAY' there. He smiled as he continued to strip before heading for the showers. Maybe he could handle a rubdown from Haskel after all.

SALMON AND RICE pilaf were on the menu that night at Chez Turner. Since cooking wasn't high on O.B.'s list of accomplishments, his fleeting thoughts of domestication were fueled by Avery's culinary abilities. He thoroughly enjoyed the meal.

After dinner, they sat on the couch and shared an ice cream sundae and a glass of wine. O.B. began to relax and let go of his apprehensions from the afternoon. Here with Avery he felt secure. But it was just a façade. He was a ballplayer and he knew there was no way he could be openly gay in the major leagues. For the moment, however, he could unwind and enjoy the peace and sense of freedom.

O.B. put his empty dish on the coffee table and sat back on the sofa. "The other night at the restaurant, you said Jason was your ex?"

Avery put his own dish on the table and leaned against O.B. "Uh huh," he responded, sounding peaceful and relaxed.

O.B. didn't want to pry, but he also wanted to know more about Avery.

"So, what happened? You don't have to tell me if you don't want to, but—"

"No, it's okay, "Avery said, shifting slightly.

O.B. laid his arm across Avery's chest, kissed the top of his head, and waited for Avery to start.

After a time Avery began. "Jason and I met about six years ago. I was new in town and just starting my job at WQBX. He had just bought the restaurant. Several folks from the station and I went to the grand opening. Since one of the guys did the entertainment and food segment on the show, we got the VIP treatment. Jason came over to the table and introduced himself. It was instant electricity. I went home with him that night. By morning I was pretty sure I was in love with him."

O.B. rubbed Avery's chest lightly.

"We continued seeing each other. I'd been staying in a hotel looking for an apartment. After about three weeks of dating, he invited me to live with him. So instead of getting a place of my own I moved in with him."

"So what happened?" O.B. asked.

"I guess it was too quick. We never did work through what we expected from a relationship. After a few months Jason started talking about three-ways. I wasn't into that, but for his sake I tried it."

"And you didn't like it?" O.B. asked when Avery paused.

"Well, it wasn't that I didn't enjoy it, but somehow I felt left out and that Jason was more interested in the new playmate than me. He told me I was being silly and backed it up with better-than-usual lovemaking when we were alone. But some-how once we introduced someone else into the relationship it seemed different. It became a point of contention. Then he started seeing guys on his own. He said he loved me, never seemed to want to break off our relationship, but just wanted the freedom to see other people. Eventually I couldn't take it any more and we parted. I got this place. We loved each other—still do I suppose, but we just had different ideas of what a partnership meant. To be fair, there was never a time when we sat down and said out loud we were a couple. I guess I took it for granted that we were, since we were in love and living together. For me it meant an exclusive commitment to one another. For him it meant something different."

O.B. mulled over what Avery had shared. He tried to put himself in Jason's shoes. Jason evidently enjoyed variety in his sex life. He had no reason to hide his sexuality, so he was free to live that lifestyle. He hadn't needed an exclusive relationship. O.B. felt a kinship with the handsome restaurateur.

O.B., too, enjoyed a varied sex life. Up to that point he'd been a one-nighter kind of guy, never allowing himself to feel anything much more than lust for his sex partners, and rarely considering seeing a guy more than once. Now the fates were aligning themselves to change his life. Once the piece on him aired tomorrow on the evening news, he'd be forced even more deeply into the closet if he wanted to preserve his career in the major leagues. He glanced down at Avery snuggled against him and once more lightly kissed the top of the man's head.

O.B. asked himself if he'd be satisfied with a monogamous relationship. The last couple of days with Avery had been great. He'd liked the attention, the lack of pressure to get the sex on and over with, and the fact that he didn't have to guard against being recognized. He could be O.B. Benson, pro ballplayer, not "Mr.-Sam-Smith-not-married-Jones," as that kid Chuck had called him the other night. Most of all, he liked Avery. But did he like him enough to get into a relationship that was more than what they had now? O.B. let that thought play on his mind as he lay back on the couch with Avery against him, Avery's hand lightly running along his muscular thigh.

O.B. came to a conclusion. At this point a committed relationship with Avery would be the result of the situation he found himself forced into because of the interview, not the result of a mutual desire for a shared life. It would be a default arrangement, a consequence of fate, and that wouldn't be fair to either of them. He sighed and put his thoughts on the subject aside.

"You ever read the *Lord of the Rings*?" Avery asked.

"Huh?" O.B. grunted, caught off guard.

"The books by Tolkien, about the rings of power?"

"No, never read the books, but I seen the movies." O.B. replied, somewhat embarrassed at his lack of literary experience.

"Well, Hobbits, you know the little people in the story?

O.B. nodded.

"They like to have second breakfasts. They're kind of into eating," Avery explained.

"Uh, yeah," O.B. answered, wondering where this was going.

"I'm kind of Hobbit-like. I'd like a second dessert."

"I'm pretty full, but if you'd like another bowl of..."

"Not that kind of dessert," Avery said, sitting up, turning, and slipping to the floor. "This kind."

Avery spread O.B.'s legs, unzipped and opened his jeans. He then pulled out O.B.'s flaccid but awakening cock. He looked up and winked, then swallowed the rapidly-inflating organ until his face was buried in O.B.'s thick pubic bush.

O.B. groaned and said, "I think I likes these Hobbitses."

O.B. KNOCKED ON the door to Avery's apartment. When Avery had invited him over for dinner again, this time to watch his interview on the evening news, O.B. had insisted that *he* would make dinner. Since he couldn't cook worth a damn, he stood waiting for the door to be opened, a salad in a plastic foam container sitting on top of two stacked pizza boxes balanced in one hand, a six pack of beer dangling from his fingers. He repeated his knock.

The door opened.

"Pizza delivery for Turner," he announced, walking past

Avery, giving the man a peck on the cheek as he made his way to the kitchen. "Hi, Coco," he said as the calico cat came running to greet him. "I got somethin' for you, too."

O.B. put the pizzas, beer, and salad on the table. "I got a meatlovers and a Hawaiian. Oh, I got us a taco salad, too. Hope that's okay? That ain't gonna be too weird with the other stuff, is it?" Without waiting for an answer, he took a bag of cat treats from his pocket and looked over at Avery. "It's all right, ain't it?" he asked, holding the bag up while Coco circled his legs, indicating that as far as she was concerned, it was certainly okay.

Avery smiled and nodded. "Sure."

O.B. ripped the bag open, poured a couple of treats into his palm, and knelt down. Coco sniffed the offerings but didn't take them.

"She'll only eat them off the floor or in her bowl. I've never gotten her to take anything from my hand."

But evidently O.B. had the magic touch, as Coco took one treat after the other from his outstretched hand.

"Well, I'll be damned," Avery said in surprise.

O.B. smiled and stood up. He took two beers out of the carton, put the remaining four in the fridge, and turned on the countertop TV while getting napkins from the holder. Retrieving plates from the cupboard and knives and forks from the drawer, he set the table. Finally he turned to Avery, who was leaning against the doorjamb watching the proceedings with a smile. O.B. gave a low bow and announced, "Dinner is served."

Avery, still smiling, said, "You certainly have made yourself at home."

Feeling embarrassed at his presumption of familiarity, O.B. stammered, "I...I'm sorry, I just thought—" Avery laughed, walked across the room, and wrapped his arms around the ballplayer. He insinuated his tongue between O.B.'s lips, and delivered several kisses while dropping his hands to massage the big man's firm ass.

"No, no, I meant it in the most positive way," Avery said

when he broke his kiss. "I'm happy you're that comfortable here. *Mi casa es su casa, amigo.*"

O.B. tightened his hold on Avery and kissed the man again. This was the fourth night he'd been with Avery—a record for sure. Yet he felt no sense of boredom or need to move on. He smiled. "Thanks," he said, giving Avery another kiss. "Let's eat. I'm starved."

THEY LAY TOGETHER after having another round of very satisfying sex. O.B. was on his back, Avery facedown next to him, a leg draped over O.B.'s, an arm over his chest. O.B. stared at the ceiling.

The pair had watched the interview as they'd eaten. O.B. had been amazed at his reaction to the fact that now even though more people in the city would recognize him, he was calm. Maybe it was that he'd had four days to adjust, to let it sink in that his life would be changed. Maybe it had something to do with the man who lay by his side.

O.B. took a deep breath and stroked Avery's hair, then kissed the top of his head. What would this turn of events have been like if the man doing the interview had been straight? He certainly wouldn't be lying here now, calm and peaceful. He probably would be raging at God and the universe for unfairly limiting his life. Instead he was feeling something akin to relief.

He'd been with Avery several times. Each experience had been better than the last. His feelings for the man had progressed from mere lust for a sexy body, to appreciation of the man's kindness and understanding of his situation, to something O.B. hardly wanted to admit to himself—affection. He not only relished the physical acts of sex, but also the conversations and camaraderie. O.B. truly liked Avery for who he was, not just for the sex—something he hadn't experienced before with a man.

But how far did he want this to go? How far could it go?

How far did Avery want it to go? Before he could begin to contemplate answers to these questions, Avery stirred and started nuzzling O.B.'s furry chest, seeking out and finding his hair-shrouded nipple. Avery began sucking on it, sending signals to O.B.'s cock that round two was about to begin. Avery raised his leg and pressed it against O.B.'s balls, gently massaging them with his thigh.

Avery slid down O.B.'s torso, swirling the mat of hair with his tongue, probing the deep navel and burying his face in the thick pubic bush. Finally grasping the erected cock, he licked his way from base to tip before swallowing it. O.B. groaned.

After several minutes of Avery's ministrations to O.B.'s dick and balls, Avery shifted position, turning around and crawling on top of the ballplayer so his own hard rod was above O.B.'s mouth as he straddled the big man's chest. O.B. kissed the tip with its pearl of pre-cum. Opening his mouth, he engulfed Avery until the man's nuts were pressed against his nose. He released the cock and maneuvered the ball sac with his tongue until both stones were inside his mouth and he could massage them with his tongue. Avery sat up and kneeled over O.B., giving O.B. access to his ass. O.B. spread the smooth cheeks and plunged his tongue into the puckered hole as far as he could, all the while kneading Avery's glutes, appreciating the man's firm muscularity.

O.B. heard the tearing of a foil wrapper and felt Avery roll the rubber on his dick. Then Avery turned around and, still straddling the big man's chest, smiled down at him. Avery positioned himself over O.B.'s pole and guided the swollen member in as he rocked back on his haunches. O.B. continued to caress and squeeze the mounds of flesh where their two bodies came together.

O.B. looked up to see Avery lean down and brace himself on his arms. Lips met and tongues danced within each other's mouths. O.B. felt his cum boil in his balls and rush to spew into the condom that separated him from being totally united with

Avery's body.

Avery sat up and pumped his dick until he shot his warm, milky fluid onto O.B.'s chest and stomach. Then he stretched out on top of O.B. and they kissed once again.

"Avery," O.B. said, emotion surging up within him. "I—I—"

Before he could try to express what he was feeling, Avery silenced O.B. with a kiss. O.B. wrapped the man in a tight hug and kissed him back.

Chapter 4

THE THUNDERBOLTS WERE in pretty good spirits. They were on a five-game winning streak. It was the longest series of back-to-back wins of the season. If they could keep up a good win-to-loss ratio for the rest of the season, O.B. knew they could squeak in at least a wildcard spot in the playoffs. The team was hoping for a win later that night in the final game against the Rays, and another sweep.

Jake Robinson walked over to O.B. in the locker room before the game. "Since we're takin' off for Baltimore tomorrow, bunch of us are going out tonight. Be a nice way to celebrate a pretty fuckin' successful home stand before we go on the road. You haven't been hanging out with us for a while. Why don't you come along?"

O.B. had been thinking about the road trip. He'd been looking forward to it. Once he was out of town he figured he could sneak off to a couple of gay bars and get some action.

Away from home he'd still be pretty anonymous. But during the past twenty-four hours he'd started having thoughts about Avery and being away from him. He'd planned on spending his last night in the city with the reporter.

"I—I don't know. I been kinda busy the last couple days, I'd like to rest up."

"Uh oh. Sounds like he's got something goin' on, don't it, fellas?" Neil Carter sang out.

"One last dip in the pussy pool for the road, huh, Benson?" another player added.

"Yeah, O.B., Where you been disappearin' to after the games the last few days?" Neil asked.

O.B. felt himself turning red.

"Hey, looks like we hit a nerve," someone laughed.

"Been a long time since you hung out with the team, O.B.," Jake said. "Come on. It'll be fun."

"Hey, O.B.," a teammate yelled to him. "Are you afraid you'll get mobbed by autograph seekers if you're seen in public now that you're a big TV star?"

"Fuck off," O.B. growled good-naturedly.

"Yeah, Benson, now you're gonna have your own bunch of groupies followin' you around and hopin' to get in your pants," another called out.

O.B. winced but forced himself to laugh along with the others.

"My turn tonight," Neil, who'd also been interviewed by Avery, added to the amicable banter. "I'm gonna be on the evening news."

"Oh my God," someone said loudly. "Once your mug goes viral it'll drive the fans away."

Everyone joined in the teasing and laughter.

"Hey, did that fairy, Turner, try to jump your bones, Neil?" someone yelled.

"Naw, he was a perfect lady," Neil called back, laughing.

O.B. felt himself tense.

"I think he liked O.B. better," Neil said, still laughing.

"How about it, O.B.? You two seemed to hit it off all right? He try anything with you?"

Feeling threatened, O.B. changed the subject: "Where you guys thinkin' of goin' tonight? Maybe I *will* come with ya."

THE BOLTS WON the game, sweeping their second series in a row. Because they'd had such a turn-around in their past few games and were on a winning streak, there was more than the usual throng of reporters in the locker room after the game.

The more O.B. thought about not seeing Avery because he'd agreed to go out with the team, the more he regretted his decision.

Maybe I can drive over to his place after I go out with the guys, he thought. O.B. looked at the crowd of reporters and players, trying to find Avery, hoping to get a chance to speak with him. O.B. finally located the reporter among a group of media types doing a Q-and-A with Whitey Woodson, the team manager.

Walking to the edge of the group, O.B. tried to get Avery's attention without looking too obvious about it. He glanced around the room nervously to see if any of his teammates were watching.

Damn it, Avery! Look over here! he thought, getting more and more frustrated.

Finally Avery turned in O.B.'s direction, a big smile flashing across his handsome face. He waved and started pushing his way through the horde of journalists, cameras, and microphones. O.B. closed his eyes and took a deep breath. An image of an old commercial where two lovers run in slow motion across a field of flowers into each other's arms came to mind. A swoop of panic swept his body. He looked around the room again. No one seemed to be paying any attention.

"Hey, O.B." Avery reached out and squeezed O.B.'s shoulder, causing the ballplayer to tense. He must have realized what was going through O.B.'s mind and dropped his hand. "Last night before you go on the road, want to do dinner again tonight?

"Um, that's what I wanted to talk to you about. I uh—" O.B. spoke softly, his eyes darting. "I'm goin' out with the guys to celebrate the streak."

Avery looked somewhat disappointed, but his smile remained in place. "That's okay. I was hoping we could get together before you left, but I understand."

"Well," O.B. dropped his voice even lower. "I'd like to come over after—if that's all right?"

"Sure," Avery said, his smile never faltering. "See you when you get there. I'll leave the door open in case it's late and you can just slip in." He winked.

O.B. had the distinct impression the words "slip in" had more than one meaning. He felt his dick twitch.

"Thanks," he said. Then, not wanting to draw any undue attention to their conversation, he nodded at Avery and added softly, "See ya later."

Avery winked and turned back to the interviews, which now focused on Jake Robinson, who had once again saved the game with some spectacular plays at shortstop. He'd also hit two home runs.

O.B. slipped away from the group and made his way to his locker.

"Hey, O.B.," Neil said, emerging from the shower room. "Saw you talkin' with Nelly over there. What did she want? Was she asking ya out on a date?" Neil smirked.

The now-familiar fear of taint by association, and the simultaneous urge to defend Avery by punching Neil in the face, reappeared.

"Give it a rest," O.B. said, trying to keep his voice neutral. "The guy just wanted to know if I was getting any response to my interview from last night. Yours is on tonight. He'll probably want to ask you the same question tomorrow."

"Then I'm glad I'm goin' out of town," Neil said, looking in

Avery's direction with a sneer. "Then he won't be able to get to me. Just being near him makes my dick shrink." Neil walked to his locker.

O.B. looked over at Avery in the crowd of reporters and sighed.

O.B. LAY ON his back staring at the ceiling. Avery was snuggled against him, head on his chest, one leg draped over his. Coco was nestled on O.B.'s other side. It was the perfect picture of domestic bliss. And a big contrast to the life O.B. had been living.

Day after day, as the week had unfolded, O.B. found himself experiencing feelings and emotions he had never allowed before. Avery had gone from being a good fuck to a guy who was fun to be with, to someone O.B. now cared for—cared for more than he wanted to admit.

But now, as the effects of the beers at the restaurant abated and his overactive libido cooled following the great sex he'd just had, the memories of the events of the day came flooding back, along with a distinct sense of confusion.

He thought back to just after the game when he'd wanted to talk with Avery. He felt he had to be so covert in doing so that he panicked if he thought anyone was watching. Then he remembered Neil's homophobic comments.

And then the restaurant. The team had gone to Jason's. Of all the places they could have chosen, the guys picked the one owned by Avery's ex-lover. To make matters worse for O.B. and his paranoia, Jason came over to their table to chat with the team. He had greeted O.B. by name. O.B. held his breath, sure that Jason would ask him how Avery was doing. Since Avery and Jason were still friends, O.B. was sure Avery had shared some of what they'd been up to the past few days. To his relief, Jason didn't make any reference to Avery. Nevertheless, O.B. didn't relax until the man left the group after saying the next round of drinks would be on him.

The worst experience of the whole night came when O.B. excused himself to go to the bathroom. He'd pissed and was standing at the sink washing his hands, aware that someone had come in and was standing behind him at one of the urinals.

"Hello there, 'Mr.-Sam-Smith-Not-Married-Jones'," a somewhat familiar voice said.

O.B. whirled around.

Chuck, O.B.'s fuck from the previous Saturday night, turned from the urinal, his semi-hard cock hanging out of his pants. "Really enjoyed seeing your interview on the news last night. So this is your big secret Mr. Smith-Jones. You're O.B. Benson, a closeted, queer major league baseball player." He walked toward O.B., his small dick bobbing tantalizingly up and down. He laughed. "When I saw you on TV, I thought, 'damn, I've been fucked by a celebrity.'" Chuck must have seen the panic on O.B.'s face, because he added, "Don't worry, Sam. I'll keep your dirty little secret."

He tucked his prick into his pants, zipped up, walked to the sink next to O.B., and washed his hands.

O.B. was frozen in place, his heart thumping with terror; his public and private lives had finally met up with each other.

"I was really excited when I saw you come in with the team. You busy later? Remember you said if we ran into each other we could maybe—" Chuck asked as he dried his hands. Then he turned and looked directly at O.B.

The ballplayer took Chuck's words as a challenge, as if he were daring O.B. to decline the invitation. O.B. knew he couldn't appear vulnerable, so, despite his inner turmoil, he forced an attitude of casualness and control. "Yeah, I am busy. Sorry, kid, this ain't your lucky night. I'm on my way out of town for a road trip."

O.B.'s show of dominance seemed to bring about a change in Chuck's demeanor. "I thought we hit it off the other night— like there was a connection between us. I'd really love to see you again. Maybe when you get back?" He asked in a manner that acknowledged O.B.'s authority.

"Maybe," O.B. replied, still feeling uncomfortable. "Gotta run. Nice to see ya again."

He ruffed Chuck's hair and walked out of the bathroom, mustering up as much swagger as he could.

EVEN HERE IN the safety of Avery's apartment, O.B.'s heart still pounded as his memories of the day began to fade.

O.B. made up his mind. He couldn't do this. As much as he was beginning to have feelings for the man sleeping at his side, as much as he'd like to explore what a life with Avery might be like, he couldn't. It wouldn't be fair to Avery or himself to live a life of secrecy and deception. No, it would be better to just leave things as they were. He'd get what action he could while out of town and once in a while maybe he'd stop in to see Avery. Besides, he didn't know how Avery felt about him. *Hell, he hasn't said anything to make me think he's feelin' anything other than that I'm a good fuck.*

Just then, Avery stirred, tightened his grip on O.B., and mumbled in his sleep, "I love you."

Chapter 5

O.B. WALKED INTO Grand Central. After winning the first road game against the Orioles, he'd gone back to his hotel, hopped on the internet, and Googled *Gay Bars in Baltimore*. Grand Central looked to be a likely spot to find a partner for the night. It was far enough away from his hotel that he wasn't likely to run into any of the other players on their way out for a night of celebrating. There was a team curfew he had to worry about now that they were playing away from home, but the bar was reported to be big enough and with a sufficiently varied clientele that he shouldn't have any trouble carrying out his plan for the evening—quickly hooking up and getting his dick into some hot guy's ass.

His eyes adjusted to the semi-darkness as he entered the club. He headed for the bar. There he ordered a drink and, as he had so many times before, surveyed the room, seeking out a potential partner for an evening of heated, anonymous sex. This would be the first time he had sought out sex since he'd been with Avery. Something inside him seemed to be trying to send a message—*think about this O.B., think about Avery. Do you really want to go back to this?* He forced his mind away from the thought, tossed down his drink more quickly than he should have, and ordered a second. O.B. knew he should go easy on the alcohol. There was a game the next afternoon. He also needed a clear head to pick a safe fuck for the night. But he wanted to silence the little voice that was trying to remind him that Avery had opened a door to a different expression of his gay life. A couple of drinks, he reasoned, wouldn't hurt his game and would put to rest those just-beneath-the-surface suggestions that he was changing in some way.

Finishing his second drink, again more quickly than he usually did, he stood and surveyed the action on the dance floor.

"Hey, big guy," came a deep voice.

O.B. turned to see a tall, burly, handsome man walk up and lean against the bar beside him. He had blue eyes, sandy blond hair, and an inviting smile.

"Hey, yourself," O.B. said, giving the man an appraising look. Obviously well-muscled and large, he wasn't O.B.'s usual choice for a sex partner. He preferred to be the bigger man in the situation. This guy was at least as big as O.B. and maybe even a little heavier. He also had a fringe of sandy hair protruding from the neckline of his shirt. O.B. preferred his men smooth.

The hunk signaled the bartender that he should bring him a drink and a refill for O.B. Having already had two drinks, O.B. was about to refuse when the man asked in his deep, sexy voice, "You're new here, aren't you? Name's Bob, by the way." He stuck out his hand.

What the hell? O.B. thought. *He's hot, I'm horny.* And, although he didn't let the idea fully form in his mind, Bob was very different from Avery.

"Yeah, I'm in town for a couple of days on business," O.B.

said, smiling and accepting the drink the bartender placed before him.

"What business you in?" Bob asked. "Sorry, I guess I didn't catch your name."

The game was on. O.B. knew "Bob" probably wasn't the guy's real name. He noted the ring finger on Bob's left hand had a tan line where a ring would be. *Married*, he thought.

O.B. took a sip of his drink and joined in the well-choreographed maneuvering as he had so many times before. "You can call me Sam, and I'm in the sports equipment business, sales rep for Wilson."

"Really?" Bob replied. "Yeah, I could tell you had something to do with sports with a body like yours." He smiled and the tip of his tongue lingered on his lips before he raised his glass to his mouth.

"You're pretty well put together yourself," O.B. said, thinking the game was moving pretty quickly and feeling pleased that it was, knowing he had to make curfew. "What do ya do for a living?"

"Concrete. I replace concrete drives, sidewalks, that kind of thing. Get a good workout tossing chunks of old pavement around." Bob smiled and unashamedly flexed a bicep, which O.B. had to admit was fairly impressive.

O.B. chuckled to himself at the display. This was what he needed—just two hunky gay guys out for a night of non-committal sexual fun.

Just then the DJ's voice came over the PA system.

"Okay, dudes, time for one of the most popular competitions here at Grand Central. The wet undies contest!"

There were cheers, hoots, and applause.

"So you guys who pack a load in your whities, get ready to show it off and win yourself a free night for two at Celie's Waterfront Inn. Strip down to your briefs and get up here on the stage!"

Bob surprised O.B. by reaching down and cupping the

ballplayer's ample package. "Man, you'd win in a walk with equipment like this. Go on, man, enter."

O.B., having just enough juice in his system to reduce his inhibitions, returned the favor and gave Bob's plentiful basket a squeeze. "I'd rather we just had our own private face-off," he replied with a leer.

"Sounds good to me," the big man responded.

Bob threw a couple of bills on the bar and turned for the door. O.B. followed. Once in the parking lot, Bob asked, "You got wheels?"

"No, came in a cab."

Bob didn't say anything, just walked across the lot to a minivan that fairly screamed "family man." O.B. smiled as he hopped in on the passenger side and buckled his seatbelt.

Bob didn't ask the usual "My place or yours." He just pulled out of the lot and headed down the street. After a short ride, during which Bob made small talk by lamenting the loss of the Orioles to the Thunderbolts, which made O.B. smile, they pulled into a Motel Six. They didn't stop at the office but made straight for a room.

Had the evening pretty well planned, eh, Bobby boy? O.B. mused as Bob slipped the keycard into the slot and they entered a room that smelled slightly of cigarette smoke despite the No Smoking sign on the door.

The door had barely closed before Bob turned, grabbed O.B. by the shoulders, and slammed him against the wall. Smashing his lips against O.B.'s, he rammed his tongue into O.B.'s mouth. O.B. felt the man's fully erect cock press against his own rapidly-hardening dick. He wrapped his arms around Bob's waist and pushed back into the assault, thinking, *Yeah, this is what it's all about—mano to mano raw sex. No frills, no gentle sweet crap, just brute force and lust.*

Bob swung O.B. around and, not breaking the mouth-to-mouth connection, pushed him back toward the bed. O.B. fell backward onto the mattress. This was going in a different direction than he'd anticipated. O.B. was usually the aggressive one. He lay there for a second, fighting the effects of the three quick drinks, trying to find a way to even the playing field and let Bob know he wasn't a subordinate bottom-boy.

Bob stood over O.B., pulled his T-shirt off over his head and flexed his hard, sandy hair-covered pecs in a show of masculine dominance. Then he kicked off his shoes, unbuckled his belt, and shoved his jeans to the floor. He stepped out of them and began fondling his abundant package through his white briefs.

"Want this, baby?" he asked in his deep, seductive voice. "Come on, daddy wants you to wet his whities and eat his cock."

O.B. didn't move. He just stared up at the blond Adonis, trying to get his bearings. O.B.'s dick was straining against the confines of his clothing. He wanted the sex, but not on these terms.

He sat up. Bob, taking this as a signal that O.B. was going to gratify his demand for oral sex, stepped forward and put his hands behind O.B.'s head and tried to force O.B.'s mouth onto the rock-hard bulge in his briefs.

O.B. threw Bob's hands off of him and stood up, facing the man, who now wore a quizzical expression.

O.B. now put *his* hands around Bob, one on the back of the man's neck and one on the small of his back.

"Let's get some things straight here, buddy boy," O.B. said with authority. "I want to have sex with you, but I ain't no bottom, and you ain't my daddy."

Bob smiled. "Well we got us a little problem then, friend, cuz I'm no man-cunt either."

Both men reached down and began massaging the others' butts while grinding their hard cocks together.

"Too bad," O.B. said. "This is one prime piece of meat."

"Yeah, you, too," Bob agreed. "You sure you've got a virgin ass? I'd sure like to be the first to plough this baby."

O.B. thought of the few times he'd agreed to be fucked. He'd never liked it. Never understood what a guy got out of it. The pain and the feeling that you had to take a shit never appealed to him.

"Took it up the chute a couple a times," he admitted. "Not my thing, though. You?"

"Never even let anyone try," Bob said in almost an arrogant tone, still kneading O.B.'s firm glutes. "How about sucking? You suck?"

O.B. confessed he did. When Bob pressed him, O.B. also admitted that he swallowed, too. O.B. was beginning to feel like they were a couple of teenagers exploring sex for the first time, instead of the hunky experienced men they were.

In the end they tried a little sixty-nine. While O.B. found Bob's thick cock to his liking, ultimately the experience wasn't all that fulfilling. Finally the two lay side by side on the bed and just jacked off.

To O.B.'s dismay and confusion, when he came close to climax all that filled his mind were thoughts of Avery and the times they'd been together. And when he did reach his peak, strong feelings of longing and affection for the man he'd left behind flooded his being. He had to bite his tongue to keep from calling out Avery's name.

The two men lay silently for a few minutes after both had shot their loads. O.B.'s main thought now was to clean up and get out. Bob, or whoever he really was, wasn't a bad guy, just a mistake. But it was the nature of the mistake that had O.B. feeling that he needed space and time to sort things out in his head.

"Want to shower?" Bob asked.

O.B.'s abs and chest were covered in cum. He rarely regretted the size of his loads or the distance he could shoot them, but this was one of those times. He was a mess and he knew he should take a shower.

"Yeah, I guess," he said, his reluctance to share the experience with the hunky blonde causing him further bewilderment.

They got out of bed and headed for the small bathroom. O.B. pissed first, got in the tub, pulled the shabby shower curtain closed and turned on the water. Bob joined him when he'd finished using the can, and the men began soaping each other. There was no question of Bob's masculine endowments. But O.B. just couldn't get into them. He needed to answer the question in his mind—was his dissatisfaction at sex with Bob the result of the guy not being his type, or did it have something to do with Avery and what had happened between him and O.B. the past week at home?

O.B. perfunctorily washed Bob's body, ass, cock, and balls. While Bob's prick responded to the stimulation, O.B. offered no encouragement to further sexual interaction.

They got out of the shower, dried each other, and dressed.

At the door to the room, Bob put his arms around O.B. "Sorry we weren't a match. You got a killer body. Wish we could of enjoyed each other more." He gave O.B. a hug.

"Yeah, well, sometimes it works and sometimes it don't," O.B. replied, feeling guilty for not being a better sex partner.

"Can I give you a lift back to wherever you're staying?" Bob offered.

O.B. declined, saying he'd call a cab.

They left the room and said goodbye in the parking lot with another awkward hug. As O.B. watched Bob drive away, he took a deep breath, pulled out his cell phone and called for a taxi.

"YOU SEEMED OFF today," Hank Petersen, the pitcher for the game that day, said as the men stood in the showers after the Thunderbolts narrow three-to-two win over the Orioles.

"Yeah, I just couldn't get my head into the game, I guess," O.B. replied.

"Probably didn't get any action last night," Neil Carter chimed in as he walked up and turned on a shower. "Look at his dick, looks kinda droopy and sad."

"How come you're so interested in Benson's dick?" Hank teased.

"Who's interested in Benson's dick?" Jake Robinson asked as he came into the shower room and turned on the spray.

"Neil," Hank said laughing. "He thinks O.B.'s dick looks droopy."

"You gotta do something to take care of that, Carter," Jake said, joining Hank's chiding of the right fielder. "Maybe a quick blow job would stiffen it up."

"Fuck off," Neil said. "I ain't no fuckin' queer!"

O.B. could see Neil was turning red.

Both Hank and Jake laughed and continued to tease. Neil continued to bluster and deny any attraction to O.B.'s or anyone else's male anatomy.

Neil, his homophobia, and his interest in O.B.'s cock were last on the list of things O.B. wanted to deal with at that moment. O.B. hadn't played well and he knew it was because he hadn't resolved the issue of why he couldn't get into sex with Bob the night before.

He needed a plan. O.B. always felt better if he had a plan when he was faced with a situation where he wasn't comfortable. He needed to figure out if it was just because Bob wasn't the usual kind of guy that turned him on or if it was something else, something with more far-reaching consequences. As the warm water cascaded over his tired and aching body, O.B. leaned his head against the tile wall and tuned out the voices of Neil and the other players.

Did his lack of enthusiasm in his encounter with Bob have to do with Avery? That was the crux of the matter that needed resolving. The only way O.B. felt he could determine that was to try again with someone else. Someone more to his taste in a fuck-buddy: Smaller, more submissive, someone with whom O.B. could again be the dominant alpha male. He would cruise again, but not here in Baltimore. He would wait until their three-game series was over and try again in Cleveland, the next stop on their road tour. He wished New York was on the list of places to play. There was plenty of gay action in that city. But

Cleveland would have to do. He needed answers and he needed them soon.

O.B. LEANED BACK against the seat of the Fiat 500. He looked at the profile of the man he'd just picked up—or who'd picked him up, depending on how you looked at it.

After surfing the web back at his hotel he hadn't had much hope of furthering his plan for clarification here in Cleveland. None of the dozen or so bars listed on the Gay Cities site had had sterling reviews, and some had been downright disgusting. But he needed closure, so he'd taken the bull by the horns and had set out.

The first bar he'd visited had been so bad he'd made an abrupt U-turn and walked out. He'd felt like he needed a shower after only being in the place for thirty seconds.

O.B. had tried two more bars and had been on the brink of giving up when on entering the fourth bar he'd literally bumped into a very handsome young man who was on his way out.

"Don't bother," the stranger had commented.

O.B. had looked in through the open door, then had turned and walked out with the guy.

Serendipity. That's the word O.B. now used as he rode with Rod to his apartment. They both had nearly given up their quest to find a partner for the evening. They happened to cross paths at just the right moment. Rod was about thirty, O.B. guessed, handsome and well put together. Shorter and less muscular than the ballplayer, Rod seemed to have all the qualities O.B. required to further his experiment. Rod even had his own place where he lived alone, so the task of anonymously finding a motel for the tryst was circumvented.

When they arrived at the stylishly-decorated residence, Rod asked O.B. if he'd like a drink.

Déjà vu. O.B.'s mind flashed back to the night Avery had

invited him home and had offered him a drink as well.

"You don't happen to have a cat, do you?" O.B. asked Rod.

"No." Rod looked confused. "My ex-boyfriend had one. But he took it with him when he moved out after we broke up. Why do you ask?"

"Nothing, just wondering."

"You a cat lover?" Rod asked as he fixed drinks at the wet bar.

"Sort of," O.B. said, thinking of Coco back home. *Home? No, Avery's apartment wasn't home.* O.B. corrected his thinking. *Back at Avery's place.* "A friend of mine has one."

"I'm thinking of getting another one," Rod said. "I kind of miss Stanley. Uh, that's the cat. Not my ex."

They both laughed.

Rod handed O.B. his glass and sat next to him.

As they sipped their drinks, O.B. kept testing the waters. Rod was attractive. He was obviously into O.B., expecting that the two of them would have sex. As they continued to talk, Rod ran his hand up and down O.B.'s thigh. O.B. felt a tingling in his groin but not the overwhelming urge he'd expect from not having had sex in several days and being with a guy whose physical attributes usually were a turn-on.

"Let's go in the bedroom and get comfortable," Rod suggested, getting to his feet, taking O.B.'s empty glass, and putting it along with his on the glass-topped coffee table.

Rod held out his hand to O.B. Taking the proffered hand, O.B. got to his feet and looked down into the smaller man's eyes, which were bright with anticipation. O.B. put an arm around Rod's waist and cupped the man's chin with his free hand. The kiss they shared was good. Rod was a way-above-average kisser. O.B. felt Rod's firm chest against him, Rod's burgeoning cock pressing against his thigh as he slipped his tongue into Rod's waiting mouth. The kiss deepened, but all O.B. could think of was Avery—how Avery would feel in his arms, how Avery's kiss was superior to Rod's, how much he longed for Avery to be the one who, in just a few minutes, would be naked on the bed waiting to unite with him. O.B. realized he'd gotten the answer he was looking for. It wasn't just that Bob wasn't his type. Rod was exactly the kind of guy that did it for him, but Rod wasn't Avery. It was Avery O.B. wanted.

O.B. stepped back out of Rod's embrace.

"Something wrong?" Rod asked, a tentative smile on his lips.

"Hey, man. I'm really sorry," O.B. said, his head reeling. This was a situation he'd never dreamed he'd ever be in—about to turn down an opportunity to have sex with a hot man because he had feelings for someone else.

"Is it something I did?" Rod asked, looking bewildered.

O.B. felt he had to explain. But being so new to these feelings he hardly knew where to begin. "Look, it's not about you. It's about me. Sit down."

Rod sat, still looking confused.

O.B. took a deep breath, sat next to Rod and looked around the room, trying to organize his thoughts. "For me, it's always been all about the sex—at least it was. And you're really hot and, well, I want to have sex with you, but—"

Rod waited as O.B. struggled with trying to explain what he didn't really understand himself.

"There's this guy back home—"

"Your boyfriend?"

"No."

"Partner?"

"No. Shit!"

Rod put his hand on O.B.'s leg.

Reassured by the man's touch, O.B. looked at Rod and continued. "I don't know what he is to me. I thought he was just a guy I know, but I never felt like this. I just know that I can't. Even though you're really a hot guy and—I want to." O.B. shook his head. "I just can't."

Rod laughed softly.

"What?" O.B. asked, feeling embarrassed.

"I know exactly what's wrong," Rod said, smiling at him.

"You do?"

"You're in love."

"I am?" O.B. said, his tone reflecting his astonishment.

"Yeah, you are. Does he know you love him?"

"How could he? I didn't know I loved him until just now when you told me I did."

Rod laughed again. "Does he love you?"

O.B. thought back to the night when, in his sleep, Avery had mumbled, 'I love you.'

"I'm not sure. I think maybe he does."

"Then just tell him how you feel. Is there a problem with that?" Rod asked innocently.

Is there a problem with that! Is there a problem with that! Hell yeah, there is! O.B.'s brain went into high gear. He got up and started pacing the floor, running a hand through his hair. *I'm a major league baseball player. Being gay in the majors isn't allowed. No way! You're not allowed to be in love with a guy, not allowed to have a relationship. It don't work that way. You'd have to hide it, sneak around to see each other. Sooner or later you'd be found out. Your career would be over. That's why I hide and sneak around*—a thought had suddenly struck him. He stopped pacing and stared at the wall in front of him, his mouth open. *That's why I hide and sneak around to have sex with complete strangers! Fuck!*

O.B. closed his eyes and let the full force of his epiphany hit him. It's no different either way: Whether it's Avery or some nameless guy, I still have to sneak around. Except that bein' in a relationship with someone ya love and care about has meaning, purpose. It's not just empty, mindless, anonymous sex. If you're gonna run the risk of getting caught and tossed out of the league, then it should be for more than an empty one-night fuck with a guy ya don't care nothing about and will never see again in your whole life.

O.B. laughed. "Man, what a fool I've been," he said out loud.

"What?" Rod asked. "Tell me what you're thinking."

O.B. turned to the man, reached down and pulled him to

his feet and hugged him. "I'm thinkin' that you're one smart, handsome fella, and I hope you find a cat that will make you very happy."

Rod shook his head and laughed. "You're crazy!"

"Maybe I am, but right now I gotta go make a phone call."

He hugged Rod once more, gave him a hard kiss on the lips and headed out the door, leaving Rod laughing and shaking his head.

O.B. pulled his cell phone from his pocket as he almost ran down the hall. On the way down in the elevator he speed-dialed Information to call a cab.

As he waited for his ride outside the building, he took a deep breath and pressed Avery's number in his contact list.

Come on, come on, he thought impatiently as the phone rang several times. Then came Avery's voice.

"Hi, this is Avery. I can't come to the phone right now, but I'd appreciate it if you'd like to leave a message. Please wait for the sound of the beep."

Shit, the frickin' answering machine!

O.B. waited for the beep. When it came he opened his mouth, but didn't know what to say. He'd been ready to tell Avery how he felt. But now the moment had arrived, he realized he couldn't use voicemail to convey such an important message. "Um...hi, uh..." *Fuck!* "This is O.B. Um, call me. I got somethin' I really need to talk to you about."

He disconnected the call just as his cab arrived. All the way back to the hotel he sat holding the phone, hoping it would ring. He rehearsed over and over just what he would say to Avery when the man called. He kept making revisions every time he went through the imaginary speech.

As O.B. walked through the lobby, several of his teammates greeted him. He nervously engaged in small talk. All the while he kept glancing at the phone still held tightly in his hand, willing it to ring while at the same time hoping he'd get to the privacy of his room before it did.

When he finally reached his room, Jake Robinson was there,

stretched out on one of the beds, watching the evening news.

Crap! How could he have forgotten he had a roommate! He couldn't talk here. Without saying a word to Jake, he turned to leave.

"O.B.?" Jake called to him as he opened the door.

O.B. turned back.

"Something wrong?"

"Uh, no. Just need to…I forgot to get…uh…need some Tums. Stomach's upset."

Shit, that's smooth, Benson! he told himself.

"I think I got something in my bag, hold on." Jake got up and walked over to his duffel.

O.B. stood, half in and half out of the room, not knowing what he'd do if Jake came up with something for his imaginary stomachache.

"Oh, sorry," Jake eventually said. "Guess I don't."

Relief swept over the catcher as he mumbled, "That's okay. Be right back."

Stepping into the elevator, O.B. took a deep breath and tried to calm down and think. *If this is what bein' in love is like!* The door slid open and he stepped out into the spacious lobby. Alcoves with comfortable chairs and couches were arranged in groups so people could sit and visit. He chose a corner where he hoped he wouldn't be disturbed. After checking for the umpteenth time that his phone was set on ringer, O.B. laid it on the arm of the overstuffed chair and closed his eyes.

Why doesn't he call? O.B. kept asking himself. I hope he's all right. Maybe he's been in an accident. O.B. checked his watch. He's fine. Still early—probably out for the evening. Maybe he's at Jason's?

O.B. picked up his phone, called Information, and got the number of the restaurant. He dialed it and waited.

"Hello, this is Jason's, how may I help you?" came a sweet female voice.

"Um, hi. I need to talk with Jason if he's available."

"Just a moment, I'll see if I can find him," came the reply. Can I tell him whose calling?

"Uh, yeah, this is O.B. Benson."

O.B. waited impatiently. *I shouldn't of called. Maybe Avery's tryin' to call me right now. No, I got call waitin'. It'd beep if he was.* He tapped his fingers on the arm of the chair as he waited.

"Hi O.B., this is Jason. What can I do for you?"

"Hi," O.B. said. "I been tryin' to find Avery. He don't happen to be there?"

"Sorry, no. In fact he hasn't been in since the night he was here with you."

"Oh, okay. Thanks."

"If he comes in—any message?"

"No. Thanks, bye."

O.B. felt foolish for making the call. What must Jason have thought of him? He tried to put that out of his mind and relax.

He'll call as soon as he gets home. Maybe he'll think it's too late. Wonder if I should call his cell? No, if he's out and with someone we couldn't talk anyway.

O.B. scrolled through his contacts and punched Avery's home phone number again. The voice message played in his ear. The beep sounded. "Hi. Me again. Uh, I'll be up for a while so you can call me anytime." Then he thought of the upcoming game, curfew, and his need to rest. As much as he wanted to talk to Avery, he knew he had a responsibility to the team, so he added, "If it gets too late, I'll turn off the phone and you can leave a message and I'll call you in the mornin'."

That base covered, he leaned back, closed his eyes, and tried again to relax.

"Benson?"

O.B. opened his eyes and sat up. It was Whitey Woodson.

"Oh, hi," O.B. said, getting to his feet, flustered by the unexpected visit from his manager.

"Whatta ya doin' up? Shouldn't you be in your room? Almost curfew."

"Yes—uh, yes, sir. But I'm expectin' an important call. And I didn't want to disturb Jake. He's a light sleeper."

"Well, don't stay up too late. We got a game tomorrow, ya know."

O.B. assured Whitey he was well aware of the game and the time. He told him it would only be a while longer.

They said goodnight. O.B. sat back down, stretched out his legs, checked the phone once again, laid it on his chest, and closed his eyes again.

From somewhere far away O.B. heard the strains of *Take Me Out to the Ball Game*. He wondered for a moment where the sound was coming from. Then he realized it was his phone. The song was his ringtone. He bolted upright, grabbed the device, and yelled, "Hello."

"Hello, this is Evan Taylor calling on behalf of the Republican National Committee—"

What the fuck! O.B. thought as the robocall droned on. He hung up.

Almost immediately his phone rang again.

"What!" he shouted into the receiver.

"O.B.? Are you okay?" This time it was Avery.

O.B. took a deep breath then smiled. "Hi, yeah, I'm fine—now that it's you."

"Good. Your messages sounded like something was wrong. Things are going all right?" Avery sounded relieved.

"Couldn't be better," O.B. replied, relishing the sound of the man's voice.

"You said you had something to talk with me about?"

Once again, O.B. hesitated. Despite his rehearsing what he would say, now that he was confronted with actually saying it, it didn't seem right to just blurt out that he loved Avery over the phone. O.B. wouldn't be able to follow up the declaration with actual physical contact. "Ah, yeah, I do. But—" An idea popped into his head. "I know this is a lot to ask, and really short notice—" *This is crazy*, he thought. He screwed up his courage and went on. "Is there any way you can fly up and meet me in Detroit? That's where we play next."

Avery chuckled. "I'm a sports reporter, remember? Don't you think I'd know where the team I'm covering is playing?"

O.B. laughed as well, but then asked nervously, "Yeah well, how about it? You think you could get the station to send you up? If not, I'll pay the airfare."

"Must be something pretty important you want to discuss," Avery said, curiosity in his voice.

"Yes, it is."

"I don't know. I could try and persuade the boss it would be a worthwhile trip as the team is doing so well."

"We don't have a game on Thursday," O. B. interjected, his excitement growing at the prospect that Avery could get away. "We don't start the series with the Tigers till Friday. I can tell Whitey I need to visit my great Aunt Tillie or something and we can stay overnight at the—whatever the hotel is at the airport."

"The Westin," Avery supplied. "And I didn't know you had a great Aunt Tillie."

O.B. started to explain that he didn't really have an Aunt Tillie when he realized Avery was teasing him. How distracted was he that he couldn't tell that Avery was making a joke? He changed gears and said, "How about it? Will you come?"

Avery laughed. "You sound pretty pumped about whatever this is you want to tell me. Any chance you'll give me a clue as to what it's all about?"

O.B. stopped to think. He needed to be, wanted to be, face to face with the man if he was going to take a step as big as this in his life. He felt he needed to say something. He thought some more. "Hmmm? Let's just say I had one of those 'aha' moments."

"Concerning?" Avery asked.

"That's all you're gonna get for now," O.B. said with a warm laugh.

"Okay, you win," Avery said. "I'll let you know tomorrow if

the boss okays the idea."

"Great!" O.B. said happily. "Can't wait to see you."

"Me, too," Avery added.

They said goodnight. O.B. took a deep breath and sat for a few moments to let the conversation replay in his mind. He was going to tell a man that he loved him. He smiled, got up, and went to bed.

Chapter 6

O.B. NERVOUSLY PACED the floor of his suite in the Westin. Avery's plane would arrive in about a half hour. Up to that point O.B. had only had excited, happy anticipation for the moment he would hold Avery in his arms and announce, "I love you." He'd never said those words to another person outside his family. No, that wasn't exactly true. He'd said it lots of times in high school and college without meaning it, when he'd been trying to get some sexy chick to put out for him. That was before he'd come to the conclusion that he liked sex with guys way more than with girls.

Then, once he'd made that discovery and the transition to sex mainly with men, to say *I love you* to another guy seemed weird. So he never had used those words, never considered feeling anything close to love for another man—until Avery.

He loved Avery. O.B. knew that for certain now. And he wanted to tell him. He would offer his body to Avery along with his declaration. It would be the first time he'd have sex with someone who he was fully conscious he loved. No, they wouldn't have sex, they'd make love. In some bizarre way he felt like a virgin, like this really would be his first time. O.B. smiled at the thought.

Suddenly O.B. had doubts. What if Avery didn't feel the same way? He hadn't really considered that before.

He did say "I love you" that night in his sleep.

Yeah, but how do I know he meant me?

He hugged me tight and said it. Of course, he meant me.

He could have meant Coco.

Don't be a shithead. He loves Coco but you don't hug a guy and think of a cat! He meant me.

That debate settled, O.B.'s mind went in another direction.

So, I tell him I love him and he says he loves me and...and what? We fuck and then...then what? Do we move in together? Or just love each other and go about our business as usual? What the hell does it mean for my life that I love him?

A knock on the door put this mental discussion on hold with no answer to that question.

O.B. took a deep breath, checked himself in the full-length mirror that hung in the entryway and opened the door.

Avery stood in the hallway, smiling. O.B. smiled back. He looked deeply into Avery's eyes, trying to gain some hint as to what the man—to whom he would in just a little while confess his love—might be feeling for him.

"Well?" Avery asked with a chuckle. "Are we going to stand here and stare at each other? Are you going to let me in so I can kiss you, or am I going to have to do that out here in the hall?"

O.B. shook his head to rouse himself, then laughed. "Oh, sorry. I. It's just so fuckin' good to see ya. Yeah, come on in."

O.B. stepped aside and let Avery pass before closing the door. Avery dropped his backpack, stood his suitcase up, and stepped into O.B.'s arms. He tilted his face up. O.B. wrapped him in a tight embrace and kissed him, feeling a deep rush of arousal.

"Can't tell you how much I missed ya," O.B. said as he broke the kiss and looked once more into Avery's eyes.

"I've missed you, too," Avery said, snuggling into O.B.'s powerful chest and tucking his head under O.B.'s chin. "I was hoping you'd call."

"You were?" O.B. asked, feeling a surge of relief that what he was about to reveal might be welcomed and reciprocated.

Avery nodded.

"Come in here," O.B. said, pulling back and leading the way into the living room of the luxury suite, anxious to put his plan for the evening into motion.

"Nice place," Avery said, looking around the spacious, expensively-decorated room. "Oh, what's this?" he said, pointing.

A silver ice bucket stood on the mahogany coffee table with the neck of a bottle of champagne protruding from the top. Two burning candles sat beside the container, their flickering light reflected in the metal. Two long-stemmed glasses were next to them.

O.B. smiled sheepishly. "Just a little something to help us celebrate."

"What are we celebrating?" Avery asked, looking pleased but puzzled.

"Well, for starters, this."

O.B. pulled Avery into another powerful embrace and kissed him, trying to communicate his new-found feelings of love through the union of their lips and the dancing of their tongues.

When they broke apart, Avery looked at O.B. with the same quizzical expression. "Do you know something I don't?"

O.B. took a deep breath. He had planned on their sharing a glass of champagne before he made his announcement, but this was it. The moment had presented itself. "Sit down."

The men sat facing each other on the couch. O.B. took both of Avery's hands in his and bowed his head.

"I'm not sure where to start or how to explain this, but—" All his practiced speeches escaped him. So he looked up and just spoke from his heart. "Since I been on this road trip I've done a lot of thinkin'." He swallowed. "And I discovered somethin'."

Avery sat quietly, waiting for O.B. to continue. When he didn't, Avery asked, "What did you find?"

"I found out I love you and want to be with you." There, he'd said it.

O.B. scanned Avery's face, looking deeply into his eyes, trying to gauge the man's reaction.

Avery sat for a few seconds, just looking at O.B., his mouth slightly open. O.B. couldn't read his expression. Was it pain in the man's eyes?

Avery dropped O.B.'s hands, got up, and walked over to the big picture window that looked out onto the tarmac. He stood with his back toward O.B., who remained on the couch, bewildered at Avery's response. Finally O.B., too, got up and went to the window.

Standing behind the man he loved, O.B. lightly placed his hands on Avery's shoulders. Avery sighed.

Avery turned and looked up into O.B.'s face. There were tears in his eyes. O.B. didn't know what to think or say. Were they tears of joy or— He put one arm around Avery's waist, the other on the back of his head and pulled him into a hug. O.B.'s heart was pounding. Had he done something wrong?

Avery shuddered. Almost too softly for O.B. to hear, he whispered, "I love you, too."

O.B. pulled back and looked down at the man, joy swelling in his heart. But Avery wasn't smiling. He was crying.

"I don't understand," O.B. said. "If you love me, why are you upset?"

Avery sighed again, stepped away, and turned back to the window. "I love you, O.B. But I don't want to. I'm afraid to."

O.B. waited for Avery to say more.

"Yes, O.B., I love you," Avery said as if confirming the emotion in his own mind. "I'm pretty sure I have from the first night we were together. But—" Avery turned around and faced O.B.

again. "I've been burned before. I told you that once I made the commitment to Jason, I expected fidelity and I got hurt."

O.B. was beginning to comprehend. He sensed what was coming next.

"You're a player, O.B. Benson: a no-strings-attached kind of guy. You've got a résumé of one night fuck partners a mile long."

O.B. swallowed hard. Images of nameless faces, anonymous cocks, and unidentifable asses flickered through his mind.

"Until a couple of weeks ago you had no intention of limiting yourself to one man or settling down. Then the interview we did went on air and your fear of exposure came into the picture. You knew your freedom was compromised."

"Yeah, but I realize now that that kind of life isn't what I really—" O.B. began to say, trying to explain that his love for Avery had nothing to do with his freedom being placed in jeopardy.

"No, let me finish," Avery interrupted. "I don't know if you can change, and I don't know if I'm willing to take that chance."

O.B. saw an opening. Avery sounded as if he wasn't sure. "But we love each other," he said, cupping Avery's chin in his hands. "You just told me you loved me since our first night together and now that I know I love you, I don't understand why we can't be together—why you don't want to be with me." O.B. floundered.

"I didn't say I didn't want to be with you, and I do love you. But love isn't always enough," Avery said with a sad smile. "I'm afraid of being hurt—again."

O.B. dropped his hands.

Avery continued. "As long as our love was unexpressed, and I didn't expect an exclusive relationship, it worked for me. But once we cross that threshold into the realm of telling each other how we feel, it changes things in my mind. I know some guys can be in a relationship and still play around. It doesn't seem to affect what they have together or their love for each other. I guess I'm not wired that way. Once love is involved, monogamy is the name of the game for me. Jason loved me and I loved him, but he needed more than I could give him physically. When he went out to get what he needed, it devastated me. I think it would be the same with you."

"No, I—you don't understand. Let me explain," O.B. said, a feeling of desperation stealing over him. He needed to persuade Avery that now he'd discovered love, he was willing, even eager, to give up his past life of meaningless sexual encounters. "Come here, sit down." He led Avery back to the couch.

The two men sat side by side. Avery looked at O.B. while the ballplayer stared at his hands that were folded between his knees. O.B. tried to bring the swirl of thoughts racing through his mind under control so he could find the words to convince his man that this was different. He turned to face Avery.

"You're not just a safe haven for me to have sex. I mean—" He swallowed. "It's not my bein' scared of bein' caught and outed if I keep sleepin' around. It really is because I realize I love you and want us to be together."

Avery didn't say anything.

O.B. went on, trying to find the right way to say what he felt. "See, when I got to Baltimore I met this guy. Bob. I think that was his name. Anyway, he wasn't my type and I couldn't—well, I could but I didn't want to. And I didn't know why. I thought maybe it was because he was too big. Shit, not that his cock was too big—it was pretty nice, but that *he* was too big. Damn!" He knew he was babbling. "Do you understand any of this?"

Avery shook his head.

O.B. stopped to gather his thoughts before plowing on once again. "I decided I might not have got into him cause he wasn't my type, but then I thought maybe it had something to do with you. Am I makin' *any* sense yet?"

Avery shrugged his shoulders and said, "No, but go on."

O.B. rubbed his forehead, trying to find a way to explain. "So, I thought I'd do an experiment."

"An experiment?" Avery asked skeptically.

"Uh, yeah. A test, you know, to see."

"To see?"

"To see if it was because of you that I didn't want to do it with Bob."

"Okay," Avery replied, not seeming to quite grasp what O.B. was trying to tell him.

"So when I got to Cleveland I picked up this guy who was more like you, and I found out I couldn't get it on with him either. So I knew."

"You knew?" Avery said slowly.

"Well, I didn't know, but he did."

"He knew what?" Avery returned. He seemed thoroughly lost.

"He knew I was in love with you. Well, not the *you* you. But that I was in love with someone. But I knew it was you as soon as he said it. And so I found out."

"You found out?"

"Yeah, I found out that I love you and want to be with you and I really want to give up all that other stuff. And it's not because of bein' afraid I'll get caught, but because of you and—"

Avery started to laugh.

"What's so funny?" O.B. asked.

"You are. You're jabbering," Avery said, putting his arms around O.B.'s neck and kissing him.

O.B. smiled. "Then you understand?"

"No, not completely. Don't give up your day job and become a TV sportscaster," Avery replied, still chuckling. "But I do understand that I love you and I think you're sincere in believing you love me."

Somewhat relieved, O.B. said, "What does that mean?"

"It means, while my mind is whispering 'don't trust him,' my heart is yelling 'I love you.' So I guess it means I'm gonna throw reason out the window and go with my heart and give us a chance."

A

LATER THAT NIGHT, O.B. lay spooned against Avery. Avery's head was cradled on O.B.'s right bicep while O.B.'s left arm was draped over Avery's chest, holding him protectively. O.B. bent and kissed the back of Avery's head. Avery stirred in his sleep and snuggled more deeply against the bigger man's body. O.B. smiled.

They'd celebrated with the champagne just as O.B. had planned. They'd discussed their future together and had then gone to the bedroom and made love. For O.B. it had been the most spectacular, most intimate lovemaking he'd ever experienced. When he was buried deep inside Avery's body, he yearned to be welded to this man, to merge their spirits and become one. O.B. had never felt anything so emotionally powerful in his entire life. The only downside had been the rubber. The feeling of the barrier between them made O.B. sad. That would have to change. He wanted nothing to come between him and his man, not even a thin layer of latex.

As reflections of their intimacy of that night still played in O.B.'s mind, he couldn't escape the fact that they hadn't yet reached the "and they lived happily ever after" stage.

Avery had made it very clear that, while he wanted to believe O.B.'s discovery had brought about an instantaneous life change, he was still skeptical. Hell, even O.B. was amazed he had experienced such a turnaround. O.B. knew he would be on probation. Avery needed to see that the leopard had truly changed his spots.

For O.B.'s part, it was very apparent from their conversation over the celebratory champagne that Avery's stance on fidelity in a relationship was paramount, and that Jason had caused a great deal of hurt when he'd begun sleeping with other men. Avery hadn't called it cheating, though. Cheating, he'd said, was when you were sneaking around behind someone's back. That was the worst kind of infidelity and almost unforgivable. In Jason's case, he was very open about his dalliances and insisted they wouldn't detract from his love for Avery and their partnership. He had even encouraged Avery to join him or find someone to play around with as well. But for Avery it was a deal-breaker.

As O.B. had listened to Avery, he'd vowed he would never do anything to cause the man the kind of hurt that Jason had. O.B. was a changed man. He would prove to Avery he was. He could accept the terms on which they would move forward: they would date, get to know one another better, and at some point discuss whether their relationship would progress to a more completely shared life. That was fair, though O.B. had already decided that the outcome would be living together. How that would square with his being a major league baseball player he didn't know. He only knew that in some mysterious, miraculous way, that would be their destiny.

"You awake?" Avery asked.

"Yeah."

Avery pressed his ass against O.B. O.B. was hard. His erection had never gone down after they'd made love.

"Come inside me again," Avery said.

O.B. didn't say anything. He just bent and kissed the nape of Avery's neck and, taking hold of his rigid cock, guided it into the man he loved.

Chapter 7

THE SERIES WITH Detroit was over and the Thunderbolts were on their way home. On the plane, the team was in high spirits. It had been a very successful road trip. They'd swept the Orioles, the Indians, and the Tigers. Those wins plus their victories over the first-place Yankees and Rays before they left had them on a seventeen-game winning streak, definitely turning their season around and probably insuring them a wildcard spot in the playoffs.

O.B. was excited, too. Not only because the team was doing so well but because he was on his way home to Avery. It had only been three days since they'd been together, but he already missed the man terribly. This was another confirmation that love had changed him. He'd never had feelings like this for anyone before.

The two had talked nightly on the phone since Avery had come to Detroit where O.B. had shared his revelation of his love. It felt good to have someone waiting for him at the end of every day to talk with and to love. He looked forward to what it would be like when he got home and they could do this face to face. O.B. knew that, for the time being, they wouldn't be living together. But at least a few times a week he would stay at Avery's and they could share their day and, he smiled at the thought, their bodies. O.B. renewed his resolve to do all in his power to prove to Avery he was a changed man and hasten the day when they would share their lives completely.

"All right, you guys! Listen up!" Whitey cut into O.B.'s reverie. "Let's cut out the booze. I got a call from the club office. We got us a crowd of fans and press waiting for us at the airport. I don't want this renewal of fan support for the team to be ruined by a bunch of wasted jocks getting off the plane and making fools of themselves. So get yourselves a cup of black coffee and use this last hour of the flight to sober up and make yourselves presentable. Carter, put a shirt on and pull your pants up." he yelled at Neil, who'd been standing in the aisle doing an impromptu striptease. "Prohibition starts now."

There was some generalized grumbling, but O.B. knew the players would do as they were told. Whitey Woodson had a firm hold on his team, and they wouldn't defy him.

When O.B. and Avery had talked the previous night, Avery had said the station would be sending a crew to welcome the Thunderbolts home. He'd also hinted that a pretty well-known reporter would be covering the story. O.B. had known that Avery meant he'd be that reporter, but he'd gone along with the tease and played dumb.

Shifting in his seat to get more comfortable, O.B. smiled at the thought of seeing Avery again. However, he wondered how the two of them would handle the situation. It would be their first real test of how to deal with their being together in a world that didn't allow such relationships without very serious consequences.

No, I'm not gonna worry about it. We'll find a way to make it work!

O.B. declared to himself. He settled back against the headrest and let happier thoughts fill his mind.

"Your boyfriend gonna be the reporter coverin' the triumphant return of the valiant warriors to the adulations of our adoring fans?" Neil Carter said as he slid into the seat next to O.B. His garbled speech testified to the amount of alcohol he'd consumed.

"What the fuck do you mean 'boyfriend?'" O.B. lashed out, immediately feeling threatened by his inebriated teammate's remark.

"Ooo, touchy, touchy. Musta hit a nerve."

"Give it a rest, Neil, you're drunk."

"Yep, that I am," Neil admitted, laughing. "But you gotta admit, you and that fairy Avery have gotten pretty close since he did your interview." Neil waggled finger in O.B.'s face as he talked. "He's always checkin' ya out after every game, mentionin' you in his news reports. I think he's got it bad for you, my friend," he slurred and patted O.B. on the thigh.

"You're imaginin' things," O.B. countered, pushing Neil's hand away. "We did the interview, got along and that's that. He doesn't pay any more attention to me than any other player on the team."

"Why? Cause your cock ain't big enough for him?" Neil giggled. "I seen your cock. It looks plenty big enough for m— uh, to me. Is the little faggot a size-queen or somethin'?"

"That's enough, you stupid asshole! Avery's a reporter. He does a good job. He's professional and his tastes in sex have nothing to do with it."

"Oh, gettin' on the *It Gets Better* bandwagon are we?" Neil continued. It seemed to O. B. that Neil was trying to push every one of his buttons.

"I'm done talkin' to you. You need to do what Whitey says. Drink some coffee and sober up. Now move, I'm changin' seats."

Neil grunted something that O.B. didn't catch but twisted sideways so O.B. could get past him. He walked down the aisle in search of an empty row of seats far from Neil.

Once settled in his new seat, O.B. tried to put Neil's remarks into perspective. The guy was a homophobe and had been on Avery's case forever. Avery was openly gay and that played into Neil's homophobic bigotry. So this was nothing new. It seemed to O.B. that Neil didn't have suspicions about O.B. being gay—just that Avery appeared to like him. But, given all of that, O.B. knew the path ahead for him and Avery was not going to be an easy one. He once more tried to put the negatives aside and concentrated on the upcoming reunion with his man.

THE TEAM STOOD in the aisle of the big jet as they were about to deplane. Whitey stood in front of them and delivered a pep talk on how they were to behave for the fans and press

"We've turned a corner. We're on the brink of a good, maybe great, season and we need to carry ourselves with the dignity required of a successful ballclub."

Fan support and respect were important to Whitey. While some on the team felt he went a bit overboard with his old-fashioned ethics and morality, no one could question his successful résumé as a player or manager. So when Whitey spoke, everyone listened and obeyed.

Whitey led the team down the passenger ramp. As they walked through the concourse, fellow travelers called out to them or pointed the team out to their children. A few people took pictures with their cell phones and some came up to ask for autographs, while others just stopped and stared.

The team left the secured area; newspeople, cameras, and a crowd of cheering fans were waiting. O.B. scanned their faces, searching for Avery.

He finally saw him. Avery was standing with his back to O.B., facing a camera with Whitey at his side. O.B. smiled, happiness filling him. He'd come home and there was someone waiting for him. Yeah, they couldn't run into each other's arms the way some of the guys with girlfriends and wives could. That would come later, when he and Avery were alone. But for now, just knowing Avery was there was enough.

"Okay, fellas," the voice of one of the PR guys broke into his thoughts. "We got your pictures for autographs. Go over to Bert there and get your pics, then head over to the fans."

The PR staff was going all out. After a dismal start to the season this winning streak was being pumped for all it was worth. Success meant money. The ballpark had been pretty empty early in the season. If the Thunderbolts kept winning, they'd draw more fans and fill more seats. They needed to garner all the fan support they could. Autographing pictures was one way to do that.

As O.B. didn't consider himself one of the more popular players, even after his TV interview, he didn't bother to head over to Bert.

"O.B.!" Bert called out. "I got a stack here for you, too."

Somewhat surprised, O.B. walked over to him, and Bert gave him a dozen or so eight-by-ten glossies and a pen. The shot showed him in full catcher's gear—without his mask—behind home plate, a big smile on his face. He was further surprised to hear several fans asking him for an autograph as he walked toward them, waiting behind the metal barriers. O.B. was a little embarrassed and more than a little overwhelmed. He was rarely recognized away from the ball field and even less frequently asked to sign anything. He pulled out a photo for a fan, barely making eye contact with him and scribbling his name before quickly moving on.

After signing five or six pictures, he felt more comfortable with the process and began to chat with his fans.

"What would ya like me to write?" he asked without looking up.

"Just write 'To Chuck, with fond memories, from Sam.'"

O.B.'s head snapped up to see a smiling Chuck standing before him.

"Hi, Mr. Smith—or is it Jones?" he said. "Nice to see you again. It's been a long time. I've missed you."

"Jesus." O.B. whispered and looked around in panic. Seeing that no one seemed to be paying attention to them, he added in an undertone, "Fuck, what are you trying to do, man, get me shut out of the league?"

Chuck laughed. "No, just wanted to get your attention."

"Well you got it. Now fuck off," he said, still keeping his voice low.

"When can I see you again? Remember you said maybe when you got back?" Chuck persisted.

O.B. felt sweat run down his back.

"Can't talk about that now," O.B. said, scrawling his name on the photograph and thrusting it back at Chuck.

"Oh, thank you, Mr. Benson. I really appreciate it. You're my favorite Thunderbolt," Chuck said loudly.

O.B. forced a smile and a thank-you to cover up their conversation and moved on to the next fan who, thankfully, was engaged in deep discussion with Jake Robinson about the Bolts' chances of making the playoffs, and had apparently not been paying attention to the exchange between O.B. and Chuck.

As O.B. distractedly continued to sign autographs, he worried about Chuck. Was he a legitimate threat not only to O.B.'s career but to his relationship with Avery? If he was, how O.B. would handle it? *I'd love to wring the little bastard's neck,* was his immediate thought.

When the media blitz was over and the team was allowed to disperse, O.B. made sure Chuck was nowhere to be seen, then looked around for Avery. His man was talking with the crew from the studio as they packed up their equipment. O.B. walked a little way over to the other side of the terminal and called Avery on his cell phone.

"Hello," came Avery's voice.

"Turn around," O.B. said.

Avery turned and walked a few feet away, making it look like he needed to be able to hear better. His smile indicated he'd located O.B. That smile seemed to calm O.B., who was still concerned and anxious over his encounter with that asshole Chuck.

"Love ya," O.B. said.

Avery smiled and nodded.

"Your place tonight?"

"That would be fine," Avery said keeping his voice detached and professional.

"What time?"

"I have to do some editing of the tapes we did today, but I should be home by ten."

"Super."

They said goodbye. O.B. stood for a few minutes watching Avery. Then he turned to make his way out of the terminal to get a cab.

"IT'S SO GOOD to have you home," Avery said as he snuggled against O.B. on the couch. Coco lay between the two men, purring loudly.

O.B. sighed contentedly. Yes. This time when Avery used the word *home*, it felt right. Here they were, his little family—Avery, Coco, and him. He knew that, just a few short weeks ago, there'd have been no way he would have dreamed he'd be doing what he was doing or thinking what he was thinking. But here he was—O.B. Benson, super stud, closeted gay baseball player, a man who had prided himself on never getting emotionally entangled with any of his sex partners—doing the domestic thing with a man and a cat. Yes, things had changed and he was glad they had.

As amazing as these revelations were, so was the fact that, when O.B. had arrived at Avery's door, they hadn't immediately ripped each other's clothes off and headed straight for the bedroom. Instead, they'd kissed each other in a tight, welcoming embrace. They'd gone into the living room, sat close together, had a drink, and talked. O.B. knew they would make love later. But just as with so many other things that had changed in the short time since he'd met Avery, also gone was the slam-bam approach to sex that had characterized his life.

Yes, Avery had made it clear they were still on a *let's see how this works out* basis. O.B. knew that meant *let's see if you can behave yourself and stick to our commitment to be faithful.* As far as O.B. was concerned, that was a no-contest.

"Want to go to bed?" Avery eventually asked.

O.B. bent and kissed the top of Avery's head. "Sure, if you're ready."

Avery answered that question by sitting up, kissing O.B. on the lips, running a hand down his chest, and giving his crotch a squeeze.

"Guess you are," O.B. said, kissing Avery back.

O.B. stood, making Coco jump to the floor with a protesting meow. He picked Avery up and started to carry him to the bedroom.

"What are you doing?" Avery asked with a laugh.

"Well, maybe I'm gettin' a little ahead of myself, but I'm carryin' ya over the threshold."

"What am I going to do with you?" Avery laughed again.

Avery shifted in O.B.'s arms. Instead of being carried like a bride, he wrapped his arms around O.B.'s neck and his legs around the ballplayer's waist, kissing O.B. as they progressed down the hall to the bedroom.

O.B. laid Avery on the bed and stood over him. Avery opened his arms and O.B. crawled on top of him, their lips and tongues finding one another, their swelling packages pressed tightly together.

O.B. rolled sideways, not breaking his hold on Avery. They lay side by side, lips and tongues seeking and finding the other's counterpart, hands roaming from shoulders to ass, squeezing, kneading, exploring.

Avery sat up and pulled his shirt over his head. Then he unbuttoned O.B.'s shirt. Avery ran his hands over the big man's massive chest, running fingers through the dense hair. Avery found and pinched O.B.'s nips, then bent to suck each in turn. O.B. moaned his pleasure and encouragement.

Pushing O.B. onto his back, Avery licked down to the waistband of the man's jeans. Then he knelt between O.B.'s legs to unbuckle his belt and undo the zipper. O.B. raised his hips so Avery could slide his jeans down, revealing his white briefs, which held captive the straining member that seemed to be Avery's goal.

Avery lowered his head and rubbed the mound of pulsating flesh with his head and face, finally mouthing the enshrouded organ through the taut cloth.

"God—Jesus—God," O.B. groaned.

He raised his hips and pushed his underwear down, took Avery's head and forced the man's face onto the rigid cock that sprang to freedom.

"Suck it, baby. It's all yours, and only yours," he moaned as the turgid organ slipped into the warm, moist confines of Avery's mouth and throat.

Avery licked, laved, and sucked. O.B. knew he was feeding copious amounts of pre-cum to his willing partner. His mind swirled with a mixture of love, lust, and need.

"Want to come this way?" Avery asked.

"No. Want to be inside you," O.B. responded, pulling Avery on top of him and kissing him.

Avery stood, took his pants and boxers off, and climbed back on the bed. He leaned over and took lube and condoms from the bedside table.

"I'm safe," O.B. said. "If you're sure you are, then we don't need 'em."

"I know I am," Avery said. "But——"

"I had myself tested after you left Detroit. I've always been careful. I don't want anything between us. Do you trust me?"

Avery hesitated for a second then tossed the unopened foil pouch onto the bedside table. "Yes." He paused for a second then said, "I trust you." He opened the lube and applied it to O.B.'s cock, which had softened a bit during their exchange.

Within seconds O.B. regained his former state of unyielding rigidity. Avery moved forward and straddled O.B.'s chest.

O.B. grasped and spread Avery's firm, muscular cheeks as Avery lowered his body and guided O.B's swollen member into his ass.

For several minutes the two held still, experiencing the union of their flesh. Then Avery began a circular motion. O.B. could feel his cock rubbing the inside of Avery's channel. O.B. slowly began to lift and lower Avery's body, thrusting his dick back and forth in Avery's hole, the intensity of the rhythm increasing with every plunge. O.B. knew from Avery's moans of pleasure he was hitting just the right spot.

After a few more minutes, Avery called out O.B.'s name, fell forward, locked him in a passionate embrace, and kissed him. O.B. could feel the warm fluids spurting from Avery's cock, coating their stomachs.

Without breaking their connection, O.B. rolled on top of his lover. Avery wrapped arms and legs around O.B. as the ballplayer buried his face in Avery's neck.

The intensity of O.B.'s thrusts increased as he neared his peak. All that mattered now was Avery and their union. When he reached his climax and spilled his seed, O.B. imagined it was love pouring from his body into Avery's.

O.B. shuddered as the last of his ejaculations subsided. He pushed himself up and looked into his man's face.

"I love you," they both said at the same time. They laughed and kissed.

O.B. slid off and lay by his lover's side. Avery turned around to spoon against O.B.'s sweaty bulk. Feeling the chill in the air, O.B. pulled a cover over the two of them and kissed the back of Avery's head. Coco jumped lightly onto the bed, found a spot behind O.B.'s bent knees, and curled up.

O.B. fell asleep to the sounds of his man's deep breathing and Coco's contented purrs.

"OKAY, I'LL SEE you at the stadium," Avery said as he kissed O.B. before heading for the door. "Thanks for feeding Coco and doing the dishes."

"It's all parta the package," O.B. laughed. "Go on, get outta here."

When the door closed, O.B. looked down at Coco, who was sitting in front of her bowl with her back to him. She looked over her shoulder and sort of yowled as if to say, "Well, you heard him, feed me."

O.B. opened a can of cat food, knelt, and scooped its contents into the dish. Coco sniffed it and gave him a look.

"Well, sweetheart, that's all there is. A minute ago you were yelling at me to hurry up—now you're gonna be picky?"

Coco flared her eyes, crouched down, wrapped her tail around herself, and started to eat.

"That's better," O.B. said with a laugh.

He poured himself a second cup of coffee and sat down to watch the cat.

He and Avery had overslept. The previous night's lovemaking had been followed by an encore that morning, after which they had dozed off. They'd slept through Coco's ritual of trying to get the humans out of bed to feed her. This had made Avery late for the morning news at the studio. A quick shower and hurried instructions were all they'd had time for.

As he sat, O.B. mused about how the day had gone so far—his first with Avery at home since his declaration of his desire to live a shared life. All this felt good, right, somehow. But O.B. knew it wasn't all candy and flowers. Avery would be at the ballpark that afternoon to cover the game, and they'd have to act like they were just acquaintances. The normal activities of a couple would be denied them. These were the very arguments O.B. had used against getting involved when wrestling with his awakening feelings for Avery. But when love had come into the picture, he knew they'd deal with the restrictions his career placed on them and somehow make a life for themselves.

Of course, there was still the issue of gaining Avery's trust, convincing the man that O.B. had truly given up his promiscuous ways and was ready to commit to a monogamous relationship. But, as far as O.B. was concerned, that was a no-brainer, a done deal.

Coco finished eating, turned, and jumped onto O.B.'s lap, head-butting his hand.

"Well, you're very welcome," O.B. said, scratching the cat behind her ears. "Come on. Just cause Daddy has to run out to work doesn't mean we have to be up. We'll do the dishes later. Time for a mornin' nap."

O.B. got up and carried Coco to the bedroom, where they lay down on the bed, the cat curled up contentedly against his chest.

Chapter 8

O.B. PARKED HIS car in the staff and players' lot and made his way to the private entrance to the stadium. A larger than usual assembly of fans was there to greet the team as they arrived to get ready for the game that afternoon.

Probably cause we're playin' better ball, O.B. thought as he made his way past them. He never paid much attention to the group as they rarely, if ever, were there to see him.

In some ways it would be easier now that he was with Avery. He wouldn't be taking a chance at being recognized as he had in the past every time he'd gone cruising. He wouldn't be doing that any longer. But he'd still have to be careful. Avery was a reporter, fairly well known in the city and openly gay. Being seen with him would be risky. O.B. hated that aspect of his new life. It was unfair to Avery to stay closeted, but the man had been nothing but reassuring when they'd discussed it. Avery'd said that having O.B. in his life meant so much that he was willing to make the sacrifice.

"Hey, O.B.—O.B. Benson," someone in the crowd called out. He turned and looked around.

"O.B. over here," came the voice again. It was Chuck.

O.B. swallowed hard and made his way over to the man. He was standing a little away from the group of fans.

"What the hell are you doin' here?" O.B. hissed under his breath when he was in front of Chuck.

"Is that any way to greet a fan?" Chuck asked with a smile.

"You're no baseball fan!" O.B. retorted. "What do you want?"

"You," Chuck said, smiling more broadly.

"I'm sorry, Chucky boy, but that's not gonna happen," O.B. said, realizing that Chuck was in a position to blow his cover and create problems.

If Avery hadn't come into the picture, O.B. might have given in to a little sexual blackmail. After all, Chuck had been a good fuck and had a great body. But now too much was riding on O.B.'s staying true to Avery to give in, if sex for silence was what was on Chuck's mind

"O.B.," Chuck said, looking around as if he was being careful not to be overheard. "I really like you. I just want to spend some time with you. Ever since that night we spent together, you're all I can think of. Is that too much too ask?"

"And if I say no?" O.B. queried. "What then, you'll let it out that I'm—" O.B. looked around and added in a hushed tone, "gay?"

Chuck looked hurt. "No, no. I've already told you I'd never do that. Honest I wouldn't. I care too much about you. Please, just a few hours with you every once in a while is all I'm asking for."

"We can't talk here," O.B. sighed. "Meet me after the game at Charlie's on Fifteenth Street. You know the place?"

Chuck brightened. "The sports bar? Yeah. Never been there, but yeah, I know where it is."

"Okay, fine. I'll see ya then," O.B. said. He turned and walked away.

Shit! Just when things were going so well, he thought as he went into the locker room.

O.B. SAT IN a booth in an out-of-the-way corner at Charlie's, waiting for Chuck to appear. Even though the Bolts had won, he felt terrible. On their first full day together as a couple, O.B. had had to lie to Avery about where he was going after the game and why he probably wouldn't be home for dinner. O.B. had made up some story about having to have his teeth cleaned. Avery hadn't seemed suspicious or even curious. He'd just said he'd see O.B. later and left the ballpark. He'd said that since O.B. wouldn't be coming home, he'd return to the studio to edit the game tapes and prepare his news report.

The catcher checked his watch. Maybe the kid wasn't gonna show. At first that gave O.B. a sense of relief. But that wouldn't really solve the problem, only put it off. O.B. and Chuck had to come to some conclusion about what was and was not going to happen between them, and they needed to talk in order to do that.

After another half hour, O.B. was about to give up and leave when he saw Chuck come in and look around. O.B. half-stood and waved Chuck over to the booth.

The kid saw O.B. and waved back, a big smile on his face.

"Sorry I'm late," Chuck said when he got to the booth and had slid into his seat across from O.B. "I missed the first bus and then got on the cross-town instead of the express and had to—"

"Not a problem, you're here now," O.B. interrupted, not really interested in the guy's excuses.

Chuck smiled broadly. "So, when are we going to get together?"

"That's not why I asked you to meet me here," O.B. replied, realizing Chuck had misinterpreted his invitation.

"It's not?" Chuck looked crestfallen.

A waiter came over to the table, and O.B. ordered another beer. When Chuck requested a Long Island Iced Tea, the waiter asked to see some ID.

Once the waiter had left, Chuck said, "I don't understand. I thought you liked me. We had a great time and—"

"Look, Chuck, it's nothing to do with you or how good we got along. I got myself a friend now. I'm kinda in a relationship." O.B. searched Chuck's face for a hint of understanding.

Chuck sat for a minute, not saying anything, just staring down at his hands. The waiter returned with their drinks. Chuck took a sip.

"Well," O.B. said, "ya gonna say somethin'?"

"Congratulations. Anyone I know?" Chuck said, disappointment in his tone.

"Yeah, probably, but I don't want to say. Just let it go at the fact I'm not gonna be cruisin' around anymore."

Chuck took a deep breath. "Okay. I'm just sorry I'm not the lucky guy."

"Look," O.B. said, not knowing exactly why he felt he needed to say something to make the kid feel better. "I did enjoy that night we had, but I met this guy and—"

"You don't have to explain. Who knows, maybe this won't work out for you. Gay relationships are famous for their fragility."

He knew Chuck was right. Gay liaisons didn't have a great track record. But he didn't want Chuck to think that what he and Avery had was something weak and vulnerable. Their relationship would be different. O.B. hid his reaction to Chuck's words.

"And if it doesn't—well?" Chuck continued and gave O.B. a weak smile. "I better get going," he said, starting to leave.

O.B. was relieved that Chuck didn't seem to be the threat he could have been. But he also felt sorry and a little guilty. He hadn't had a clue that Chuck might have had feelings for him that went beyond the sex they'd shared.

"Hey, you haven't finished your drink. And you probably haven't had supper yet. I haven't either, so let me buy you dinner at least."

"You don't have to do that," Chuck said, starting to slide

out of the booth.

"I know I don't have to, but I want to," O.B. said, reaching out and putting his hand on Chuck's.

Chuck shrugged. "Well, okay. I'm gonna warn you. If I get too drunk on these things—" He held up his drink. "You can't blame me for jumping your bones." He smiled and winked.

They ordered dinner, ate, and talked for about an hour.

O.B. drove Chuck home. Chuck gave O.B. a kiss on the cheek and squeezed his thigh before getting out of the car.

Chuck stuck his head back in the window. "Remember, I got first dibs on you if this guy doesn't work out."

"I'll remember," O.B. said with a smile.

O.B. drove off, relieved that Chuck didn't seem to be bent on wrecking his career or his relationship with Avery. *Now to get home to my man,* he thought, a warm feeling stealing over him.

He smiled and hummed along with a song playing on the radio, the lyrics saying something about makin' love the whole night through. *Sounds good to me,* O.B. mused and stepped on the accelerator.

O.B. CAME OUT the shower. He had a towel wrapped around his waist and used another to dry his hair.

The game had gone well. Hell, the night before had been good, too. He'd gotten to the apartment long before Avery had come home, so he'd figured his story about the dentist would float.

He and Avery had made love before going to sleep.

Coco had woken them early the next morning, insisting on being fed. Once O.B. had attended to the cat's breakfast, he'd returned to the bedroom where he and Avery had made love until it had been time for Avery to leave for the studio.

That cat's early wake-up call ain't so bad after all," O.B. considered, walking down the row of lockers. When he got to his own locker, Avery was waiting for him.

O.B. put on his aloof professional air and greeted the reporter. "Hello, Turner. What can I do for ya?" He followed that up with a surreptitious wink.

"Hi, Benson," Avery said in his best sportscaster's manner. "You had a good game today. I'd like to get your take on how the Thunderbolts look for taking that wildcard spot in the playoffs. You guys have been burning up the diamond the last couple of weeks. Got any idea what's behind this turnaround in the team's game?" He returned O.B.'s wink.

O.B. almost chuckled out loud at their veiled exchange.

In a quieter voice, Avery leaned forward and started to ask if O.B. planned on coming home with him that night.

"Benson!" a dripping Neil Carter said, coming around the corner of the row of lockers. He was naked apart from a towel that he was using to dry his hair. His half-staff cock swayed as he came up to O.B. and Avery. "Oh, hi, Turner," he said when he saw Avery.

Avery nodded his greeting.

"What do ya want, Neil?" O.B. asked, irritated at the interruption while at the same time uneasy that Neil might have overheard some of what Avery had said about O.B. coming home.

"Was just wondering who you were out with last night at Charlie's."

O.B. looked at Avery. The reporter's face went pale.

"Wh...what?" O.B. stammered, returning his attention to Neil.

"Last night. I saw you with some kid at Charlie's havin' dinner. Looked like one of the fans you were talkin' to before the game. Seemed like you were havin' a pretty interestin' conversation."

O.B. didn't know what to say. He felt sweat break out on his brow.

Avery stared at him. His expression was one that O.B. would never forget. It reminded him of the look of hurt you had when you discovered there was no Santa Claus or that your dog had just been run over by a truck.

"Well, gentlemen. I'll leave you to your little discussion. I need to get back to the studio and do some—uh, stuff," Avery said in a voice that sounded strained.

"Avery, I—" O.B. started, then looked at Neil, who was watching them intently.

Avery turned and walked away.

Fuck!

"Was it something I said?" Neil asked naïvely.

O.B. ignored him and dressed as fast as he could. He had to get to Avery, had to explain. *Damn you, Neil Carter. Damn you!* O.B. raged impotently. Again the curse of being gay in the major leagues reared its ugly head. There was no way O.B. could punish this fucking idiot standing stupidly before him, acting all innocent and confused without tipping his hand and raising suspicion.

He left Neil standing by the locker looking bewildered and rushed toward the parking lot. He got there just in time to see the taillights of Avery's car turn onto the main street.

O.B. PACED THE floor of Avery's living room, running his fingers through his hair with one hand while holding his cell to his ear with the other. Coco sat on the arm of the sofa, her eyes following O.B. as he walked back and forth.

"Come on, come on, Avery, answer. I can explain this. It's not what you think."

O.B. had lost track of how many times Avery's cell voicemail had answered: "You've reached Avery's cell phone. Leave a message."

This time O.B. didn't say anything. He'd left countless messages already. He didn't know what else to say. He left a text message instead. He hated texting. His fingers were so big it took him forever to get it right. But he was desperate so he muddled through.

Why didn't Avery just come home? Was it because he knew O.B. would be there and didn't want to deal with the situation?

Finally, exhausted with worry and fatigue, O.B. collapsed on the couch. Coco came and sat on his lap. She reached up and nuzzled O.B. with her nose, purring loudly. O.B. lifted the cat and buried his face in her soft fur.

"I just want him to come home so I can explain," O.B. said to the cat. "I just want him to come home."

Sometime later, O.B. couldn't tell how long, he was startled awake by the sound of the door opening. He jumped to his feet, dumping Coco on the floor with a loud mew of protest.

"Avery!"

"What are you doing here? Don't you have another dentist appointment—or would that be someone you'd like to take out to dinner?"

O.B. went to him. "Avery, let me explain. It's not what you think. The guy I was with—"

Avery backed away. "So you admit you were with someone? Once a player, always a player. Man, you must have stamina. Get some on the side and then come home to—to your what—your man-toy, and fuck him three times in one night?"

O.B. knew Avery was deeply hurt by what he imagined had happened, and he was being irrational. Otherwise, he couldn't possibly think that O.B. would be able to pull off the intense lovemaking they had shared after O.B. had been with someone else earlier.

"Please let me tell you what this is all ab—"

"What really gets me is that Jason at least waited until we'd been together a couple of months before he got ants in his pants. And even then he didn't cheat on me. You couldn't even wait until you were home a week before you went out and got your rocks off behind my back. I guess the leopard can't change his spots after all."

O.B. felt like he'd been slapped in the face. He remembered Avery's words when he'd first confessed his love and Avery had explained his hesitancy to believe such a declaration. *Cheating is when you're sneaking around behind someone's back. That's the worst kind of infidelity and almost unforgivable.*

O.B. clung to the word *almost.* It gave him a glimmer of hope. He got an idea—a crazy idea. It might be the only way he could get through to the man he loved, who was in such pain and unable to listen to anything O.B. tried to say.

"Don't go away. You stay right here. I'll be right back."

O.B. grabbed his car keys off the table next to the door and ran out of the apartment. He got in his car and drove across town as fast as he could without the risk of getting a ticket.

O.B. pulled into the driveway of a modest house in a suburb outside the city. The lights were still on inside. He checked his watch: eleven-twenty. *Probably still up watching the news,* he thought as he got out of the car, dashed up the steps to the front door, and rang the bell.

An older man—balding and stout, in bathrobe and slippers—opened the door a crack. "Can I help you?" he asked suspiciously.

"Is Chuck here?" O.B. blurted out.

"Chuck?" the man asked, seeming not to understand.

"Yeah, Chuck. This is where I dropped him off last night. Does he live here?"

"Yes, he lives here. He's my son. What do you want with him? Is he in some sort of trouble? Say, you look familiar. I think I just saw you on the news. Why, you're O.B. Benson!"

"That's right, yes, I am." O.B. tried to be polite but his patience was running thin. He had to talk to Chuck. "Is Chuck here, I really need to see him," he asked again.

"Who's at the door, Harold?" a woman's voice asked.

"It's O.B. Benson, mother. You know, the baseball player. We just saw him on the ESPN news."

"Oh, my! The baseball player! What does he want? Bring him in!"

"He wants to talk to Chuckie."

Harold gestured for O.B. to come inside. The insanity of his plan was beginning to dawn on him but he had to make

Avery understand, and this could be the only way.

O.B. came into the living room just as Chuck came down the stairs, rubbing sleep from his eyes. He was wearing only pajama bottoms, which were slightly tented in front.

"What's all the noise down here?" Chuck asked, then he spotted O.B. "What are you doing here?

"That's the second time I've been asked that question tonight. Get dressed. I need you." Seeing everyone's shocked expressions, O.B. realized they'd taken his statement the wrong way. He hastily added, I need you to talk to my boyfriend Avery. He—he—just get dressed. I'll explain on the way."

Chuck disappeared upstairs and O.B. turned to the kid's parents. They were looking at him strangely. He realized he'd probably just outed himself to them, but right at that moment he didn't really care.

O.B. shrugged his shoulders and nodded toward the TV screen. "What about them White Sox?"

O.B. OPENED THE door to Avery's apartment and literally dragged Chuck inside. Avery was sitting on the couch. Coco had been sitting on Avery's lap. She jumped down and disappeared into the kitchen. Avery slowly got up.

"What's this! You're bringing your twink trick home to meet me?" Avery said, looking Chuck up and down.

"Holy cow!" Chuck said. "You're Avery Turner, the sports guy on WQBX." He turned to O.B. "You didn't tell me your boyfriend was *that* Avery."

"Avery, this is Chuck—uh, just Chuck," O.B. said, realizing he didn't know Chuck's last name. "He's the guy Neil saw me having dinner with last night."

"I've already figured that out," Avery said as he stood waiting with a this-better-be-good expression.

"Anyway," O.B. continued, nudging Chuck forward. "Go

on, tell him."

Chuck took a step toward Avery. "Gosh Avery Turner! I watch you on the news every morning," he said sticking out his hand.

"Chuck!"

Chuck dropped his hand.

"Yeah, right, sorry. See, I was kind of stalking O.B. at the ballpark yesterday. We slept together once and I was hoping I'd get another shot at him because he's so great in bed and—but then you probably know that already."

"Chuck!" O.B. said again, exasperated.

Chuck looked back over his shoulder at the ballplayer.

O.B. rolled his eyes and said, "Get to the point!"

Chuck turned back to Avery. "He was worried I was going to out him to the team if he didn't sleep with me again. I told him no way. I like him too much to do that. I was still hoping he'd give me some bed time so I kept pestering him. But he didn't want to talk to me at the stadium in front of everyone, so he had me meet him at Charlie's to set me straight. Oops, poor choice of words." Chuck giggled.

Avery said, "Go on."

"He wanted to let me know that he had no interest in me whatsoever and to not bother him anymore because he had this fantastic guy he was head-over-heels in love with and wasn't now, or would ever be, available to me, that we were over and done with. We had dinner and a drink and he took me home. Believe me, Avery—Mr. Turner—that was it. At dinner all he talked about was you and how much he loved you, how you had changed him, and how he wanted to do everything he could to make you happy. Honest, I was hitting on him at the start, but he's really hung up on you, man."

Chuck stopped. He glanced from Avery to O.B. and back to Avery again. O.B. watched Avery, to see if Chuck's words had gotten through.

For what seemed like an eternity they all stood looking at each other. Then, without saying a word, Avery turned and walked out of the room into the kitchen. O.B. and Chuck exchanged looks. Chuck shrugged and made an I'm-sorry-I-did-the-best-I-could face. O.B. said, "That's okay," and followed Avery into the other room.

Avery stood, leaning on the counter, his back toward the door.

O.B. paused, waiting for Avery to turn around. When he didn't, O.B. said, "Avery?"

"I'm sorry," Avery said, still facing away, his head hung down.

O.B.'s heart fluttered. Was he sorry because he didn't believe Chuck, or sorry for another reason?

Avery turned to face O.B. "I'm so sorry."

In two strides Avery was across the room and in O.B.'s arms.

"I'm sorry for how stupid I was to jump to conclusions because of what that latent frickin' homo Neil said. I should have had more faith in you."

"No, no," O.B. replied. He stroked Avery's head, relief rushing through his body. "I shoulda told ya about Chuck and that I was gonna talk to him instead of makin' up some stupid story about the dentist."

"That *was* a bit lame." Avery laughed softly. He looked up into O.B.'s eyes and said, "But I should have trusted that you wouldn't hurt me that way. It's just that after Jason—well—I just couldn't face going through anything like that again, and I overreacted without thinking. Please forgive me."

"Done," O.B. said, pulling Avery into a deep kiss, which he hoped washed away any remaining doubt.

When he broke the kiss, he said, "So you think Carter's a queer, too, huh?"

Avery laughed. "Isn't it obvious? Why? You want to date him?"

"Are you fuckin' kiddin' me?" O.B. said, planting another sloppy kiss on Avery. "Come on, let's get started on our make-up sex. I hear it's the best kind."

He started to pull Avery toward the bedroom.

"Uh—what about Chuck?" Avery asked.

"Oh, yeah, Chuck. I'll call him a cab!"

Epilogue

"ARE YOU SURE you want to do this?" Avery asked as he and O.B. walked into the Out and Proud one Saturday night a couple months later.

The Thunderbolts had made it to the playoffs and O.B. wanted to celebrate that accomplishment as well as show Avery a good time.

"Yes, sir, I do," O.B. replied, putting his arm around Avery's waist and walking them toward the bar. "We can't stay cooped up in your apartment forever. Ain't natural. It's about time I took my man out and showed him off." He reached down and gave Avery's ass an affectionate squeeze.

They found a couple of stools at the bar. They both ordered beers, leaned back, and surveyed the scene. The music was playing and the dance floor was crowded.

O.B. took a deep breath and looked over at Avery, a feeling of happiness and contentment stealing over him.

What a difference from the last time I was here, he thought. That was the night he'd picked up Chuck. Back then he'd been playing a game, hiding who he was. Now he felt free. He was here with Avery and this was no charade. This was his life.

"You know—" O.B. began.

Avery turned to look at him.

"I been thinkin'. Now that you've decided *you're* thinkin' about keepin' me—"

Avery laughed and reached up to kiss him.

"I been thinkin' that my place is a lot bigger than yours. Maybe we should consider movin' you and Coco over there."

Avery became serious. "I d' love that, but that'd be a really risky thing to do. I mean, how would you—we explain it? It would be bound to make people think something was going on—ask questions. Maybe we should wait."

"I know," O.B. said. then he smiled and added, "but I suppose I could say ya were my butler and his crazy calico cat. Think that'd fool 'em?"

Avery shook his head and the two men laughed.

Then O. B. turned more solemn. He put his arms around Avery and said, "Look, I'm pretty young. I got me another ten years in the majors, maybe more if my legs hold out. After I retire I won't give a fuck who knows about us. But we can't stay closeted up *all* that time. Ten years is a long time to wait for freedom."

Before Avery could respond, a rather handsome older man came up to them. "You're Avery Turner aren't you? I watch you all the time on the morning news."

He looked at O.B. and screwed up his face as if he was trying to put a name to someone who looked familiar but he couldn't quite place.

"Hey!" his eyebrows rose in recognition. "You're O.B...."

"Hi, Sam! Hi, Avery!" came a loud voice. Chuck walked up dressed in a killer tank top and tight leather jeans. He kissed both O.B. and Avery on the cheek. "Well, Sam Smith!" he continued, slapping O.B. on the chest and winking at them. "I haven't seen you in such a long time. Still looking fit as ever. Looks like things are working out for the two of you, huh? How's the real estate business going, Sam? The market picking up any?"

Flabbergasted, O.B. looked at Avery, who was suppressing a laugh.

Chuck then turned to the man who was now giving Chuck an appraising look.

"Aren't you gonna introduce me to your hunky friend, Sam?" Chuck said, running his hand up and down the stranger's torso.

"Uh, Chuck, this is—sorry, I didn't get your name," O.B. said.

"Dan," the guy replied, not taking his hungry eyes off Chuck. "Dan Jones."

"Yeah, right," Chuck said, laughing and winking once again at O.B. and Avery. "Come on, Dan—ah, *Jones*. Dance with me and let's get to know each other better. Then you can buy me a drink later." Turning to O.B. and Avery, he said, "Bye, you two. Have fun tonight." Chuck took Dan by the hand and started to pull him away.

Dan turned back to the men. "Great to meet you, Avery. Really like your show. Sam, good to meet you, too." He stuck out a hand for O.B. to shake. "If you have a business card, I've got a couple properties I'm thinking of listing, and—"

"Oh, come on, Dan. This is Saturday night. I want to dance. That silly old business stuff can wait," Chuck said as he steered Dan toward the dance floor.

When they had gone, Avery took a deep breath and said with a laugh, "Well, thank God for Chuck. That was a close one."

"Yeah, it was," O.B. sighed and watched Chuck and Dan disappear into the mob of gyrating bodies. "But it's gonna happen sooner or later. One of these days it'll be on the news: 'O.B. Benson: First openly gay ballplayer,'" O.B. said philosophically. "Maybe you'll be the sportscaster to make the announcement." He pulled Avery into a hug.

"And you're okay with that?" Avery asked, searching O.B.'s face.

"Not really. I'd hate to be shut out of the majors because I'm gay. I love my career in baseball. But I love you more." He tightened his hold on Avery and gave his man a kiss. "If there's no way I can play and have you at the same time—well, then there's no room for O.B. Benson in the majors. Come on, let's dance."

About the Author

Terry O'Reilly is a retired school teacher living a quiet life in the Midwest with his three dogs and his horse. He began writing several years ago at the urging of a friend and fellow author. Writing has become an important part of his life, allowing him to explore his thoughts, needs, and feelings as well as learn about other cultures and eras as he researches his stories. His books were formerly published with Aspen Mountain Press, eXcessica, and Amber Allure.

For more information, visit him online at terry-oreilly.com.